COLD SERVICE

ROBERT B. PARKER

COLD SERVICE

A SPENSER NOVEL

NO EXIT PRESS

This edition published in 2007 by No Exit Press,
P.O.Box 394, Harpenden, Herts, AL5 1XJ
www.noexit.co.uk
First Published by No Exit Press in 2005

A CIP catalogue record for this book is available from the British Library.

ISBN 10: 1-84243-170-6
EAN 13: 978-1-84243-170-2

2 4 6 8 10 9 7 5 3 1

Printed and bound in Great Britain by CPD, Blaina, Wales

For Joan
far together

REVENGE IS A DISH BEST SERVED COLD

COLD SERVICE

1

IT STARTED without me.

"Bookie named Luther Gillespie hired me," Hawk said. "Ukrainian mob was trying to take over his book."

"Ukrainian mob?" I said.

"Things tough in the old country," Hawk said. "They come here yearning to breathe free."

"Luther declined?"

"He did. They gave him twenty-four hours to reconsider. So he hired me to keep him alive."

A dignified gray-haired nurse in a sort of dressy flowered smock over her nurse suit came into the hospital room and checked one of the monitors tethered to Hawk. Then she nodded, tapped an IV line and nodded again and smiled at Hawk.

"Is there anything you need?" she said.

"Almost everything," Hawk said. "But not right now."

The nurse nodded and went out. Through the window I could see the sun in the west reflecting off the mirrored surface of the Hancock Tower.

"I'm guessing that didn't go so well," I said.

"We're on the way to his house, on Seaver Street, somebody from a window across the street shoots me three times in the back with a big rifle. Good shooter, grouped all three shots between my shoulder blades. Missed the spine, missed the heart, plowed up pretty much of the rest."

"The heart I'm not surprised," I said, "being as how it's so teeny."

"Don't go all mushy on me," Hawk said. "I wake up, here I am in a big private room and you be sitting in the chair reading a book by Thomas Friedman."

"*Longitudes and Attitudes,*" I said.

"Swell," Hawk said. "How come I got this room?"

"I know a guy," I said.

"When I go down, they go on after Luther and kill him and his wife and two of his three kids. The youngest one was in day care."

"Object lesson," I said. "For the next guy, they push."

Hawk nodded again.

"Where's the youngest kid?"

"With his grandmother," Hawk said. "They tell me I ain't going to die."

"That's what I heard," I said.

There were hard things being discussed, and not all of them aloud.

"I want to know who they are and where they are," Hawk said.

I nodded.

"And I want to know they did it," Hawk said. "Not think it, know it."

"When are you getting out?" I said.

"Maybe next week."

"Too soon," I said. "You won't be ready even if we know who and where."

"Sooner or later," Hawk said, "I'll be ready."

"Yeah," I said. "You will."

"And I'll know it when I am."

"And when you are," I said, "we'll go."

We were on the twenty-second floor in Phillips House at Mass General. All you could see from where we were was the Hancock Tower gleaming in the setting sun. Hawk looked at it for a while. There was no expression on his face. Nothing in his eyes.

"Yeah," he said. His voice was uninflected. "We will."

2

I STOPPED BY pretty much every day to visit Hawk. One day when I arrived, I saw Junior and Ty Bop lingering in the hallway outside his room. Both were black. Junior took up most of the corridor. Fortunately, Ty Bop weighed maybe one hundred thirty pounds, so there was room to get by. I smiled at them cordially. Junior nodded. Ty Bop paid me no attention. He had eyes like a coral snake. Neither meanness nor interest nor affection nor recognition showed in them. Nor humanity. Even standing still, he seemed jittery and bouncy. Nobody on the floor or at the nursing station ventured near either of them.

"Tony inside?" I said to Junior.

He nodded and I went in. Tony Marcus was standing by the bed, talking to Hawk. Tony's suit must have cost more than my car. And he was good-looking, in a soft sort of way. But that was illusory. There was nothing soft about Tony. He pretty much ran all the black crime in eastern Massachusetts, and soft people didn't do that. Tony looked up when I came in.

"Well, hell, Hawk," Tony said. "No wonder people shooting your ass. You got him for a friend."

I said, "Hello, Tony."

He said, "Spenser."

"Tony and me been talking 'bout the Ukrainian threat," Hawk said.

"They come to this country," Tony said, "and they look to get a foothold and they see that nobody in America much care what happen to black folks, so they move on us."

"Got any names?" I said.

"Not yet," Tony said. "But I'm planning to defend my people."

"Tony bein' Al Sharpton today," Hawk said.

"Don't you have no racial pride, Hawk?" Tony said.

Hawk looked at Tony without speaking. He had three gunshot wounds and still could barely stand, but the force of his look made Tony Marcus flinch.

"I'm sorry, man," Tony said. "I take that back."

Hawk said, "Yeah."

"I tellin' Hawk he ought to let me put a couple people in here, protect him. Until he's on his feet again."

"Nobody got any reason to follow up," Hawk said. "They done what they set out to do."

"I think that's right," I said.

Tony shrugged.

"'Sides," Hawk said. "Vinnie's been in and out. Susan's been here. Lee Farrell. Quirk and Belson, for chrissake. There's been a steady parade of good-looking women worrying where I'd been hit. Plus, I got a phone call from that Chicano shooter in L.A."

"Chollo?" I said.

"Yeah. He say I need a hand he'll come east."

"See that," I said. "I told you that warm and sunny charm would pay off in friendship and popularity."

"Must be," Hawk said.

"Well," Tony Marcus said, "I got a vast criminal enterprise to oversee. I'll be off. You need something, Hawk, you give me a shout."

Hawk nodded.

"Say so long to Ty Bop for me," I said.

"He try to bite you when you came in?" Tony said.

"No."

"See that," Tony said. "He like you."

After Tony left, I sat with Hawk for about an hour. We

talked a little. But a lot of the time we were quiet. Neither of us had any problem with quiet. I looked at the Hancock Tower; Hawk lay back with his eyes closed. I had known Hawk all my adult life, and this was the first time, even in repose, that he didn't look dangerous. As I looked at him now, he just looked still. When it was time to go, I stood.

"Hawk," I said softly.

He didn't open his eyes.

"Yeah?" he said.

"Got to go."

"Do me a favor," he said with his eyes closed.

"Yeah."

"Have a drink for me," he said.

"Maybe two," I said.

Hawk nodded slightly without opening his eyes.

I put my hand on his shoulder for a moment, took it away, and left.

3

I WAS IN my office having a cup of coffee and looking up Ukraine on the Internet. Like most of the things I looked up on the Internet, there was less there than met the eye. But I did learn that Ukraine was a former republic of the Soviet Union, now independent. And that *kartoplia* was Ukrainian for potato. I knew if I kept at it I could find a Ukrainian porn site. But I was spared by the arrival of Martin Quirk in my office, carrying a paper bag.

"Did you know that *kartoplia* means potato in Ukrainian?" I said.

"I didn't," Quirk said. "And I don't want to."

I pointed at my Mr. Coffee on top of the file cabinet.

"Fresh made yesterday," I said. "Help yourself."

Quirk poured some coffee.

"You got donuts in the bag?" I said.

"Oatmeal-maple scones," Quirk said.

"Scones?"

"Yep."

"No donuts?"

"I'm a captain," Quirk said. "Now and then I like to up-grade."

"How do you upgrade from donuts?" I said.

Quirk put the bag on the desk between us. I shrugged and took a scone.

"Got to keep my strength up," I said.

Quirk put his feet up on the edge of my desk and munched on his scone and drank some coffee.

"Two days ago," Quirk said, "couple of vice cops are work-ing a tavern in Roxbury, having reason to believe it was a distribution point for dope and/or whores."

The maple-oatmeal scone wasn't bad, for a non-donut. Outside my window, what I could see of the Back Bay had an authentic gray November look with a strong suggestion of rain not yet fallen.

"So the vice guys are sipping a beer," Quirk said. "And keeping an eye out, and two white guys come in and head for the back room. There's something hinky about these guys, aside from being the only white men in the room, and one of the vice guys gets up and goes to the men's room, which is right next to the back room."

Quirk was not here for a chat. He had something to tell me and he'd get to it. I ate some more scone. The oatmeal part was probably very healthy.

"The guy in the men's room hears some sounds that don't sound good, and he comes out and yells to his partner, and in they go to the back room with their badges showing and guns out," Quirk said. "The tavern owner's had his throat cut. The two white guys are heading out. One of them makes it, but the vice guys get hold of the other one and keep him."

"Tavern owner?" I said.

"Dead before they got there; his head was almost off."

"And the guy you nabbed?"

"Cold," Quirk said. 'The dumb fuck is still carrying the knife, covered with the vic's blood, on his belt. Big, like a bowie knife, expensive, I guess he didn't want to leave it. And the vic's blood is all over his shirt. ME says they tend to gush when they get cut like that. So we bring him in and we sweat him. He speaks English pretty good. His lawyer's there, and a couple of Suffolk AD's are in with us, and after a while he sees the difficulty of his position. He says if we can make a deal he can give us his partner, and if the deal's good enough he can give us the people shot that family over by Seaver Street."

I was suddenly aware of my breath going in and out.

"Do tell," I said.

"I was in there at the time and I said 'family named Gillespie?' He said he didn't know their names but it was over by Seaver Street and it was the end of October. Which is right, of course. And I said, 'How about the rifle man that shot the bodyguard.' And he said, 'No sweat.'"

"He Ukrainian?" I said.

"Says so."

"What's his name?"

"Bohdan something or other," Quirk said. "I got it written down, but I can't pronounce it anyway."

"Did he give you the others?"

"Yes. His lawyer fought him all the way. But Bohdan isn't going down for this alone, and he does it even though his lawyer's trying to stop him."

"Think the lawyer was looking out for him?" I said.

"Not him," Quirk said.

"Bohdan's a mob guy," I said.

"Seems like," Quirk said.

"And his lawyer's probably a mob lawyer."

"Seems like," Quirk said.

"And you got the others?"

Quirk smiled.

"Five in all," he said.

"Including Bohdan?"

"Including him," Quirk said.

"They all Ukrainian?" I said.

"I guess so. Except for Bohdan, they all swear they don't understand English, and Ukrainian translators are hard to come by. We had to get some professor from Harvard to read them their rights."

"Maybe you should keep him on," I said.

"Too busy," Quirk said. "He's finishing a book on . . ." Quirk took out a small notebook, opened it, and read from it. ". . . the evolution of Cyrillic language folk narratives."

I nodded.

"That's busy," I said. "Can I have another scone?"

Quirk pushed the bag toward me.

"You think it'll make Hawk happy?"

"Not sure," I said.

"You think he'd rather have done it himself?"

"Not sure of that either," I said. "Hawk is sometimes difficult to predict."

"No shit," Quirk said.

4

IN THE AFTERNOON on Thursday, late enough to be dark, with the rain coming hard, I walked down Boylston Street to have a drink with Cecile in the bar at the Four Seasons. We sat by the window looking out at Boylston Street with the Public Gardens on the other side. Cecile was wearing a red wool suit with a short skirt and looked nearly as good as Susan would have in the same outfit. A lot of people looked at us.

"Hawk asked me to talk with you," I said.

She nodded.

"You know his situation?"

She nodded again. The waiter came for our order. Cecile had a cosmopolitan. I asked for Johnnie Walker Blue and soda.

"Tall glass," I said. "Lot of ice."

The waiter was thrilled to get our order and delighted to comply. There was considerable traffic on Boylston, backing up at the Charles Street light. There were fewer pedestrians. But enough to be interesting, collars up, hats pulled down, shoulders hunched, umbrellas deployed.

"I know his surgeon," Cecile said. "We were at Harvard Med together."

"And he's filled you in?"

"Well," Cecile said with a faint smile. "He respects patient confidentiality, of course . . . but I am reasonably abreast of things."

"Hawk wants me to explain to you," I said.

"Explain what?" she said.

"Him," I said.

"Hawk wants you to explain him to me?"

"Yes."

Cecile sat back with her hands resting on the table and stared at me. The waiter came with the drinks and set them down happily, and went away. Cecile took a sip of her drink and put it back down and smiled.

"Well," she said, "I guess I'm flattered that he cares enough to ask you . . . I think."

"That would be the right reaction," I said.

"I could have considered it possible that I knew him well, and perhaps even in ways that you don't," Cecile said. "For God's sake, you're white."

"That would be another possible reaction," I said.

Cecile drank some more cosmopolitan. I had some scotch.

"How long have you known Hawk?" she said.

"All my adult life."

"How old were you when you met him?"

"Seventeen."

"Good God," Cecile said. "It's hard to imagine either of you being anything but what you are right now."

"Hawk wants you to understand why he doesn't want you to visit."

"He doesn't need to explain," Cecile said.

"He doesn't want you to see him when he isn't . . . when he is, ah, anything but what he has always been."

Cecile nodded. She was looking at her drink, turning the stem of the glass slowly in her fingers.

"I am a thoracic surgeon," she said. "I am a black, female thoracic surgeon. Do you have any guess how many of us there are?"

"You're the only black female surgeon I know," I said.

"Surgery is still mostly for the boys. If you're a woman and want to be a surgeon, you need to be tough. If you are a black woman and want to do surgery . . ."

She drank a little more.

"I do not," she said, "need a man to protect me. I don't need one who can't be hurt."

"No," I said. "I think Hawk knows that."

She raised her eyebrows.

"But he needs to be that," I said. "Not for you. For him."

"That's childish," Cecile said.

"He knows that," I said.

"He could change," Cecile said.

"He doesn't want to. That's the center of him. He is what he wants to be. It's how he's handled the world."

"The world being a euphemism for racism?"

"For racism, for cruelty, for loneliness, for despair . . . for the world."

"Does that mean he can't love?"

"I don't know. He doesn't seem to hate."

"It's a high price," she said.

"It is," I said.

"I'm black."

"That doesn't make you just like Hawk," I said.

"I don't have to pay that kind of price."

"You're not just like Hawk."

"Neither are you," she said.

"No," I said, "neither am I."

"So what are you saying?"

"I'm saying he can't see you until he's Hawk again. His Hawk. And he cares enough about you to want me to explain it."

"I'm not sure you have," Cecile said.

"No. I'm not sure I have, either," I said.

"Have you ever been hurt like this?" Cecile said.

"Yes."

"Did you want to be alone?"

"Susan and Hawk were with me. But the circumstance was different."

The waiter drifted solicitously by. I nodded. He paused. I ordered two more drinks. Cecile looked out the window for a while.

"You love her," Cecile said.

"I do."

"Is there a circumstance in which you would not want her with you?"

"No."

Cecile smiled again.

"How about if you're cheating on her?" she said.

"I wouldn't do that," I said.

"Have you ever?"

"Yes."

"But you won't again."

"No."

"She ever cheat on you?"

"She has."

"But she won't again."

"No."

Cecile smiled without any real humor.

"Isn't that what they all say?"

"It is," I said.

I sipped some scotch. Rain ran down the window, the streets gleamed. The scotch was excellent.

"You're not going to argue with me?"

"About what they all say?"

"Yes."

"No," I said.

Cecile studied me for a time.

"You're more like him than I thought," she said.

"Hawk?"

She nodded.

"I have never heard him defend himself or explain himself," she said. "He's just fucking in there, inside himself, entirely fucking sufficient."

There was nothing much to say to that. Cecile drank the rest of her cosmopolitan.

"And except for being white, I think you are just goddamned fucking like him," she said.

"No," I said. "I'm not."

She was studying my face like it was the Rosetta stone.

"Susan," she said. "You need Susan."

"I do."

"Well, he doesn't need me."

"I don't know if he does or not," I said. "But not wanting to see you now doesn't prove it either way."

"If he doesn't need me now, when will he?"

"Maybe need is not requisite to love."

"It seems to be for you," she said.

"Maybe that would be my weakness," I said.

"Maybe it's not a weakness," she said.

"Maybe an infinite number of angels," I said, "can balance on the point of a needle."

She nodded. The waiter brought her another drink.

"We are getting a little abstract," she said.

"I don't know if he loves you," I said. "And I don't know if you love him. And I don't know if you'll stroll into the sunset together, or should or want to. But as long as you know Hawk, he will be what he is. He's what he is now, except hurt."

"And being hurt is not part of what he is?" she said.

I grinned.

"It is, at least, an aberration," I said.

"So if I'm to be with him, I have to take him for what he is?"

"Yes."

"He won't change."

"No."

"And just what is he?" Cecile said.

I grinned again.

"Hawk," I said.

Cecile took a sip of her drink and closed her eyes and tilted her head back and swallowed slowly. She sat for a moment like that, with her eyes closed and her head back. Then she sat up and opened her eyes.

"I give up," she said.

She raised her glass toward me. I touched the rim of her glass with the rim of mine. It made a satisfying clink. We both smiled.

"Thank you," she said.

"I'm not sure I helped."

"Maybe you did," she said.

5

•

HAWK AND I went to a meeting with an assistant pros-
ecutor in the Suffolk County DA's office in back of Bowdoin
Square. It wasn't much of a walk from the hydrant I parked
on One Bullfinch Place, but Hawk had to stop halfway and
catch his breath.

"Be glad when my blood count get back up there."

"Me too," I said. "I'm sick of waiting for you all the time."

He looked bad. He'd lost some weight, and since he didn't
have any to lose, his muscle mass was depleted. He still

seemed to walk slightly bent forward, as if to protect the places where the bullets had roamed. And he looked smaller.

The meeting room was on the second floor—in front, with three windows, so you could look at the back of the old Bowdoin Square telephone building. Quirk was already there, at the table, with a Suffolk County ADA, a fiftyish woman named Margie Collins, whom I had met once before.

"Hawk," Quirk said. "You look worse than I do."

"Yeah, but I is going to improve," Hawk said.

Quirk smiled and introduced Margie, who didn't seem to remember that she'd met me once before. Since Margie was still quite good-looking, in a full-bodied, still-in-shape, blond-haired kind of way, her forgetfulness was mildly distressing.

"Our eyewitness shit the bed," Margie said when we sat down.

"Stood up in court and said he had been coerced by the police," Quirk said. "Didn't know the defendants. Didn't know anything about any crimes they'd committed. He was our case. Judge directed an acquittal."

Hawk was quiet. For all you could tell, he hadn't heard what was said.

"How'd they get to him?" I said.

"We had him in the Queen's Inn," Quirk said. "In Brighton. Two detectives with him all the time. Nobody in. Nobody out."

"Except his lawyers," Margie said.

"Bingo," I said.

"Yeah. Can't prove it. But when we flipped him in the first place, his lawyer was fighting us all the way."

"Did I hear you say lawyers?" I said.

"Yes," Margie said. "The second one was in fact an attorney. We checked. But I'm sure he was the one carried the message."

"What does whatsisname get for bailing on his deal."

"Bohdan," Quirk said.

"He does life," Margie said.

"Which is apparently a better prospect than the one they offered him," I said.

"Apparently," Margie said.

She looked at Hawk.

"I'm sorry," she said. "We can't shake him."

Hawk smiled gently.

"Don't matter," he said.

"At least the man who shot you will do his time."

"Maybe," Hawk said.

"I promise you," Margie said.

"He ain't going to do much time," Hawk said.

Quirk was looking out the window, studying the back of the building as if it was interesting.

"They gonna kill him in prison," Hawk said. "If he gets there. He rolled on them once. They won't take the chance."

Margie looked at Quirk. Quirk nodded.

"Be my guess," Quirk said.

Margie looked at me.

"And what is your role in all of this?" she said.

"Comic relief."

"Besides that."

"My friend dodders," I said. "I have to hold his arm."

"Don't I know you from someplace?" Margie said.

"I swept you off your feet about fifteen years ago, insurance fraud case, with a shooting?"

"Ah," Margie said. "That's when. You remember that as sweeping me off my feet?"

"I like to be positive," I said.

Margie nodded slowly. Then she looked at Hawk.

"I've heard about you," she said. "You may want to deal with this problem on your own."

Hawk smiled.

"And I can't say that I'd blame you," she said. "But if you do, and we catch you, I will be sympathetic, and I will do everything I can to put you away."

"Everybody do," Hawk said.

"Meanwhile, we'll stay on this thing," Margie said. "It's a horrific crime. But honestly, I'm not optimistic. What we had was the witness."

"And now you don't," Hawk said.

"And now we don't," Margie said.

"And they been acquitted."

"Yes."

"And double jeopardy apply."

"Yes."

Hawk stood slowly. I stood with him.

"When they kill him," Hawk said. "Maybe you can get them for that."

"We'll try to prevent that," Margie said.

"No chance," Hawk said.

He turned slowly toward the door, one hand holding the back of his chair.

"We'll catch them sooner or later for something," Margie said. "These are habitual criminals. They aren't likely to change."

"Thanks for your time," Hawk said.

"I'll have coffee with you," Quirk said. "Margie, we'll talk."

She nodded, and the three of us went out. Slowly.

6

WE WALKED SLOWLY to a coffee shop on Cambridge Street. If Quirk noticed that Hawk was shuffling more than he was walking, he didn't comment.

All he said was, "You back in the gym yet?"

"Nope," Hawk said. "But ah has started to brush my own teeth."

"Step at a time," Quirk said.

We got coffee. Quirk took a thick manila envelope out of his briefcase and put it on the table.

"If I go before you do and forget this, and leave it lying here on the table, I want you to return it to me immediately. I only got two other copies. And under no circumstances do I want you to open the envelope and read its contents."

"Where my man, Bohdan?" Hawk said.

"In jail awaiting trial," Quirk said.

"Suffolk County?" Hawk said.

"Yep."

"Think he'll last till his trial?" Hawk said.

"He thinks so," Quirk said. "He thinks everything's hunkydory with the other Ukrainians."

"You keeping him separate?" I said.

"Yep."

Hawk made a soft, derisive sound.

"Never going to make trial," Hawk said.

Quirk shrugged.

"And ain't that a shame," Quirk said.

"What have you got on the rest of them?" I said.

"The details are, of course, confidential police business, which is why I have them sealed up safe in this envelope. We been talking to the organized-crime guys, the FBI, immigration. We know it's a Ukrainian mob. Which means we are dealing with some very bad people. Even the Russians are afraid of the Ukrainians."

"They straight from the old country?" I said.

Quirk shook his head.

"We think from Brooklyn. They've set up around here in Marshport, up on the North Shore, which has got a small Ukrainian population."

I nodded.

"They come in, start small. Take over a book here and horse parlor there. Usually small-time black crime. The assumption being that the blacks have the least power."

Quirk grinned at Hawk.

"Which, from the looks of you, may be correct at the moment."

"Enjoy it while you can, honkie."

"Hey," Quirk said. "I'm a police captain."

"That's right, you is," Hawk said. "Enjoy it while you can, Captain Honkie."

"Anyway, pretty soon they have all the black crime, and are moving on the Asians. And so it goes. Sometimes they end up with the city. They probably got Marshport. Boston is their first big-city try since Brooklyn."

"They don't run Brooklyn," I said.

"Nobody does," Quirk said. "But they got a part."

"This wouldn't have happened," I said, "if the Dodgers hadn't left."

Both of them looked at me silently for a while. Then Quirk shook his head.

"Gotta go to work," he said.

He stood up.

"We're going to chase these guys until we catch them for something," he said. "But if someone gets there first . . ."

Quirk shrugged.

"Well, what's a poor cop to do?" he said, and turned and went out the front door of the coffee shop. When he was gone I picked up the manila envelope.

"Hey," I said softly, "you forgot your envelope."

7

———•———

OUTSIDE THE WINDOWS of my apartment, it was
getting dark. Hawk was asleep on the bed in my bedroom.
The trip to Bullfinch Place had used up all his strength.
Hawk slept a lot. I used the couch. The couch was fine. I sat
at my kitchen counter with the overhead lights on and the
contents of Quirk's big envelope spread out in front of me.

There were mug shots and arrest records of five men:

Bohdan Dziubakevych
Fadeyushka Badyrka

COLD SERVICE

Vanko Tsyklins'kyj
Lyaksandro Prohorovych
Danylko Levkovych

All five originally came from Odessa. All five had legitimate immigration credentials. None was wanted by Ukrainian police. They were foot soldiers. There had been various arrests for assault, extortion, and racketeering in Ukraine, Poland, Russia, Romania, New York, New Britain, and Boston. No one appeared to have done serious jail time. Witnesses were probably hard to come by. The men were all between thirty-five and forty-five; they had hard, middle-European faces. Their eyes had seen awful things. I looked at the names some more and decided not to memorize them. I wasn't sure I could forget the faces.

At about twenty to six, Susan unlocked my door and came in with two large shopping bags. She was in her understated work mode—gray suit, black sweater, clear nail polish, quiet makeup.

"It's hard to shrink people," she once explained to me, "if they're fascinated by your eyeliner."

She was beautiful and quiet when she came from work. Sometimes she wasn't coming from work. Then she looked beautiful and flamboyant. She put the bags on the floor and came and kissed me.

"How is he?" she said.

"He's asleep," I said.

"Hard to imagine him tired," she said.

She looked at the pictures spread out on the counter.

"Who are those awful men?" she said.

"Ukrainian mob," I said. "The ones Hawk will be looking for when he's not tired."

"Ick," Susan said. "Can you help me with the bags?"

I put the photos and paperwork back in the envelope and put the envelope away. I picked up the two shopping bags and put them on the counter.

"Could I have a glass of orange vodka?" Susan said.

"Straight up," I said. "No ice."

"With a slice of orange," she said.

"You eat and drink like no one else I know."

"I like warm orange vodka," she said.

"My point exactly," I said.

I got her drink while she unpacked the bags. Bread, cheese, cold chicken, fruit, and two bottles of Riesling. I gave her the warm vodka, and she sipped it as she arranged the food on a couple of good platters that she had insisted I buy.

"Can he eat and drink?" Susan said.

"He's permitted to," I said. "But he doesn't have much interest in it yet."

She nodded. I made myself a scotch and soda in a tall glass with a lot of ice. We sat at my counter and had our drinks together.

"You're on the couch?" Susan said.

"Yes."

"Do I remember correctly?" Susan said. "Were we on that couch the first time we ever made love."

"I think so," I said. "At least that's where we started. I remember you burst into applause afterwards."

"Are you sure?" she said.

"You said I should get an award for sustained excellence."

"I'm pretty sure I didn't say that," Susan said.

"What did you say then?"

"I think I said, 'Never touch me again, you lout.'"

"Maybe," I said. "But you didn't mean it."

Hawk came out of my bedroom, barefoot, wearing jeans and a T-shirt. His face was still damp from washing.

"Did we wake you?" Susan said.

"I sleep about twenty hours a day," Hawk said. "Anything wakes me up is good."

"Can you eat anything?"

"Maybe sip a drink," Hawk said. "What you drinking?"

"Orange vodka," Susan said. "Up with a slice."

"Up?"

"Yes."

"Warm orange vodka?"

"Yes."

"Jesus, girl," Hawk said.

He looked at my drink.

"Gimme one of those," he said.

I made him one and he eased onto a stool at the counter.

"Would you be more comfortable on the couch?" Susan said.

"Too hard to get up."

"We could help you," Susan said.

Hawk looked at her balefully.

"Or not," Susan said.

Hawk sipped his drink. He seemed to be listening to his body as the drink went down.

"Okay?" I said.

Hawk nodded.

"Pretty good," he said.

Susan took a couple of grapes off the platter and ate them and sipped some vodka. Hawk shuddered.

"You will be all the way back sooner or later," Susan said.

"I will," Hawk said.

"And then what?"

Not a lot of people said "then what?" to Hawk. But Susan was one who could. Hawk looked at the manila envelope I had put aside. He shrugged.

"Business as usual," he said.

"You're going to find those men," Susan said.

"Yes."

"You're going to kill them."

"Yes."

"Five people."

"Four," Hawk said. "Old Bohdan will be dead long before we ready."

Susan nodded toward me.

"You will want him to help you."

"Up to him," Hawk said.

"Are you going to help him kill four people?" Susan said to me.

"I'm going to help him find them, and I'm going to help him not get killed. He'll kill who he kills," I said.

"Isn't that sort of a fine line?" Susan said.

"Very fine," I said. "But it's a line."

Susan nodded.

"That troubling to you?" Hawk said.

"Yes," she said. "It is very troubling."

"He don't have to."

"Yes," Susan said. "He does."

She looked at Hawk, holding her warm vodka in one hand and a green grape in the other. I knew she had forgotten both.

"He does have to," she said.

We were quiet. I put my hand on her thigh and patted softly. She never disappointed. She always knew.

"Ain't happening for a while," Hawk said.

Susan ate her grape and sipped more vodka.

"I know," she said brightly. "Want some chicken?"

8

HAWK WASN'T running yet. But he could walk a ways. So, in the week before Thanksgiving, we were walking with Pearl along the river in back of where I lived. Actually, Hawk and I were walking. Pearl was tearing around, looking for something to hunt or eat or sniff or bark at.

"Like you," I said. "Dark, slick, and full of energy."

"I still dark and slick," Hawk said.

It hadn't been cold enough long enough for the river to freeze, and the gray surface was ruffled with small whitecaps.

"Two out of three," I said.

We weren't passing a lot of people, but Hawk wasn't bent over anymore, and he didn't move anymore like an elderly man with bad feet.

"The blood count is creeping up," I said.

"Slow bastard," Hawk said.

Two young women ran by in luminescent tights and wool hats pulled down over their ears. They both glanced at Hawk as they passed.

"That's a good sign," I said.

"Lucky they didn't stop," Hawk said. "Best I could do is talk dirty for a minute."

Pearl had located an old french fry beside a trash barrel. She ate it proudly and came over and jumped up and gave me a kiss that smelled vaguely of fryalator.

"Tracked it down and ate it," Hawk said. "Dog's a savage."

"It's in the genes," I said.

It was midday. Traffic on both sides of the river was easy. The sun was almost above us in the southern sky. It was a pallid winter sun, and it shed little heat. But it was cheery enough.

"Quirk called me," I said. "Bohdan got it."

"Good," Hawk said.

"They were taking him from his cell down to the visiting area to see his lawyer. Two guards. They were moving some other prisoners in from the exercise yard. They passed each other. It got a little crowded for a minute."

"And somebody shanked him," Hawk said.

"In the throat," I said.

"And nobody saw nothing," Hawk said.

"All of a sudden there's lots of blood and Bohdan is down," I said. "And you're right. Nobody and nothing."

"Same lawyer come to see him 'fore he changed his story?" Hawk said.

"Quirk says yes."

"Bunch of dumb foreigners, they got some reach," Hawk said.

"They knew when the exercise was over. So they knew when the corridor would be crowded. And they had a guy there ready and able to cut Bohdan's throat."

"And they knew which guards going to be on the scene," Hawk said. "They knew they'd cooperate."

"You're not cynically suggesting," I said, "that the keepers are sometimes as corruptible as the kept?"

"Jug is its own place. Got no connection with how people live anywhere else. Everybody in the jug a prisoner. The guards just get to go home nights."

"Well," I said, "it's not like we're surprised."

"Nope."

"Leaves us four more," I said.

"If Bohdan was telling the truth."

"Instead of lying about some friends of his to get himself a deal?" I said.

"Hard to trust people these days," Hawk said.

"In which case," I said, "instead of killing him because

they didn't trust him, they might have killed him because he framed them."

"Need to know," Hawk said.

"Well, we got a list," I said.

"And we'll be checking it twice," Hawk said.

9

SUSAN HAD SPENT the better part of two days making a pumpkin pie for Thanksgiving. Obviously she was exhausted, so I agreed to cook the rest of the meal, which I began at nine Thanksgiving morning. Susan sat at the kitchen table and drank a cup of coffee.

"If you hadn't forced yourself upon me," Susan said, "you could have begun preparations much earlier."

"I know," I said. "But after dinner I'd have been too full to force myself upon you."

"Oh good," Susan said. "I can rest easy."

I had the small turkey all rinsed and patted dry.

"Will you make that stuffing with the apples and onions and little cut-up sausages?"

"Yes."

I had coffee, too, and drank some.

"Would you like to look at my pie again?" Susan said.

"I beg your pardon?"

"The pumpkin pie."

She got up and walked to the refrigerator and opened the door. The pumpkin pie was on the top shelf.

"Ta-da," Susan said.

"Did you really take two days on that thing?"

"Don't call her *that thing*," she said. "What if she hears you."

"She looks worth every moment spent on her."

Susan went back to her seat at the table. I sliced up eight small breakfast sausage links into my stuffing mix.

"What is Hawk doing for Thanksgiving?" Susan said.

"I don't know," I said. "I don't think he's got much appetite yet."

Pearl got her front feet onto the kitchen counter next to me and pushed her nose into the stuffing mix. I put her back on the floor.

"How'd she know the recipe called for dog slobber," I said.

"What recipe wouldn't," Susan said.

Pearl walked over and rested her head on the table beside

Susan and gave a gimlet eye to the plate of buttermilk biscuits I had made for us to nibble. Susan broke one in half, and handed one half to Pearl.

"Whole-grain," she said to Pearl. "Healthful."

Pearl sniffed it, accepted it carefully in her mouth, and took it into the living room and onto the couch. Susan put a minute dollop of honey on the other half and popped it into her mouth.

When she had chewed and swallowed and drunk some coffee, she said, "Is he seeing Cecile?"

"I don't know."

"Did you ask?"

"No."

Susan smiled and shook her head.

"Amazing," she said.

"What?"

I peeled two Granny Smith apples and cored them and sliced the remains into my stuffing.

"He has risked his life for you and you for him."

I turned on the water faucet and began to peel onions in the stream of descending water so they wouldn't make me cry. I didn't want Susan thinking I was a sissy.

"And," Susan said, "you are planning to risk it again."

"Prudently," I said.

"And you don't even ask him what his plans are for Thanksgiving, or if he's spending it with anyone."

I had the first onion peeled. Pearl padded back in from

the living room and sat near Susan and looked hopeful. I put the onion on the cutting board and turned and leaned against the kitchen counter and looked at Susan.

"I was walking along the river with Hawk, couple of weeks ago," I said. "And he remarked that life in prison had no connection with how people live anywhere else."

"He's probably right," Susan said.

"He's nearly always right," I said. "Not because he knows everything. But because he never talks about things he doesn't know."

"Not a bad idea," Susan said.

"No," I said. "Quite a good one."

"But what's that got to do with not knowing what he was doing for Thanksgiving?"

"I digressed," I said. "And it misled you. Go back to the thing he said about prison."

Susan poured herself half a cup of coffee and emptied in a packet of fake sugar.

"Analogy," Susan said. "Hawk's world is not like anyone else's."

I nodded.

"So asking Hawk about Thanksgiving is like asking a fish about a bicycle," Susan said.

"Or asking him about Cecile."

"Does Cecile matter to him?"

"Yes," I said.

"But?"

"But not the way you and I do."

"Who does?" Susan said.

"Good point," I said.

"Do you understand him?"

"Up to a point," I said.

"And then?"

"Hawk's black. He's been outnumbered all his life. I don't know, and probably can't know, quite what that's like."

"Or what it took for him to become Hawk," Susan said.

"And to keep being Hawk," I said. "He didn't choose a Hawk that's easy to maintain."

"But if he doesn't maintain," Susan said, "he'll disappear."

"He'd laugh at you for saying that."

"Yes," Susan said. "But it doesn't mean it's not true."

"Besides," I said. "You have a doctorate from Harvard and you live in Cambridge."

"So I'm used to being laughed at," Susan said.

10

THE WEEK AFTER CHRISTMAS, Hawk and I were at the Harbor Health Club. Hawk had been doing twenty-pound curls and hundred-pound bench presses. And resting a lot between sets. Now he was on the bicycle, with the resistance set low and the sweat running down his face.

"After the Gray Man shot you," Hawk said, "how long before you was a hundred percent?"

"A year," I said.

Hawk nodded. Henry Cimoli came over with a bottle of water and gave it to him.

"Thin and flabby at the same time," Henry said. "Reminds me of my first wife."

Henry walked over to me. His small body bulged out of his white T-shirt.

"I could probably kick his ass now," Henry said. "Be my chance."

I nodded.

"Be wise to kill him if you do," I said.

"I know," Henry said. "Eventually he'll get better."

Hawk kept pedaling.

"You so little," Hawk said, "you be punching me in the knee."

"You're so scrawny," Henry said, "that would probably drop you."

Hawk was struggling to keep his breathing normal.

"You . . . ever knock . . . anybody down . . . when you . . . fighting?" Hawk said.

"I knocked Willie Pep down once," Henry said.

"He stay down?" Hawk said.

"Not for long," Henry said. "It was the last punch I landed."

Hawk got off the bike and sat on a bench, taking in air.

"Doctor say you okay to work out?" Henry said.

Hawk nodded.

"He say do anything I can."

"Which ain't much," Henry said.

"Yet," Hawk said.

Henry nodded.

"Yet," he said.

Henry went away. I finished my set and sat down beside Hawk.

"I have been collecting data," I said.

Hawk wiped his face with a hand towel and nodded.

"I have addresses for our four Ukrainians and for the two lawyers we know about."

"Talk to any of them?"

"No."

"Good," Hawk said.

"We could, though, if you want to," I said.

"Ain't ready yet," Hawk said.

"I could sort of protect you," I said. "Unless you annoyed me."

Hawk shook his head.

"Got to wait," Hawk said.

"I could ask Vinnie to join us," I said.

"Can't have no one protecting me," Hawk said.

I spent a little time thinking about that.

Then I said, "No, you can't."

11

IN MID-MARCH I was sitting in my office, invoicing clients. It was tedious, but it reminded me of why I did what I did. Outside my window the sun was shining. It wasn't spring yet, but the snow was beginning to decay, and the sour smell of long-buried leaves bore the gentle promise of milder times.

Hawk came in. He took off his coat and folded it and put it on my client chair. He took the big .44 Mag off his belt and laid it on top of the coat. Then he dropped to the floor and did ten push-ups with his right arm and another ten with his left. Then he stood.

"Am I to gather that you're ready?" I said.

"I am."

Hawk put the .44 back in its holster and put his coat back on.

"Now?" I said.

"Un-huh."

"You got a plan?"

"Start with Tony," Hawk said.

"Marcus?" I said.

"Want to find out what's been going on since they shot me."

"And Tony will know," I said.

"'Course he will," Hawk said.

"His interests are the same as ours," I said. "He could help."

"He will," Hawk said. "If we need him."

I heaved a big sigh.

"Back down to the ghetto again," I said.

"Good for you," Hawk said. "Give you a chance to be a minority."

"I like you," I said. "I am a minority."

"Just 'cause I recovered," Hawk said. "Don't get sloppy and emotional."

"My car or yours?" I said.

"I be embarrassed to show up at Tony's place in your ride."

Tony Marcus had an office in the back of a restaurant and nightclub at the edge of the South End, which had been called Buddy's Fox. Then Tony hired a marketing consultant and the place was now called Ebony & Ivory.

"Swell name," I said as Hawk parked across the street. "Implies elegant racial intermingling."

"Except you the only ivory I ever seen in there," Hawk said.

There were booths along both walls, a bar across the back, and a narrow corridor to the right of the bar that led to washrooms and Tony's office. In a booth near the door, Junior and Ty Bop looked at us when we came in. Ty Bop was drinking coffee. Junior simply sat. Neither of them said anything. The patrons ignored us. The bartender nodded as we walked by.

"Hawk, my man," Tony Marcus said when we went into his office. "You are looking buff."

"Lost that unhealthy pallor," I said. "Hasn't he?"

"And you ain't," Tony said to me.

I grinned.

"I back in business," Hawk said. "Want to talk about the Ukrainians."

"Figured the time would come," Tony said. "'Less you died."

"Time has come," Hawk said. "What you know?"

"I know they here," Tony said. "I know they costing me money. I know the connection runs back to Brooklyn, and probably back to Ukraine, wherever the fuck that is."

"Even further than Brooklyn," I said.

"You not a candy cane," Hawk said to Tony. "Whyn't you chase them out."

"They don't come at you direct, man. They pressure a

pimp, or one bookie, or a guy doing drugs in one neighbor-hood. When the one guy cracks they move in big, and then to get them out you got a damned war. It costs you money. The cops come looking. The feds get involved. Prosecutors are RICO this and conspiracy that. It's still easier to work around them."

"You think they stop?" Hawk said.

"No," Tony said. "They want it all."

"So you going to have to step up sooner or later," Hawk said.

"They also pretty bad," Tony said.

"That so?" Hawk said.

"You should know," Tony said.

"Why Gillespie come to me?" Hawk said. "Why didn't you protect him?"

Tony looked at the ceiling above his desk for a while. He had short salt-and-pepper hair and a big moustache. He had on a tie, as he always did. His shirt was immaculate. His suit fit him perfectly. He was even a little soft around the neck as befits a successful middle-aged executive.

"Luther and I were, ah, in disagreement," Tony said.

"You thought he holding out on you?" Hawk said.

"I did."

"So you left him on his own?" Hawk said.

"I did."

"Mistake," Hawk said.

Tony nodded.

"But I cut a guy off, I can't go bailing him out later, you unnerstand. I do that, pretty soon everybody be trying to fuck with me and I have to do some major bang bang."

"Many of the people they've moved in on been in disfavor?" I said.

"Disfavor." Tony shook his head. "Man, you white folks do talk funny."

"Were they?" Hawk said.

"Couple were," Tony said. "Some of the others weren't mine."

"I thought they were all yours," I said.

Tony smiled.

"They were going to be," he said.

Hawk took out the paper on which I had typed the names of the four Ukrainians that Bohdan had named.

"Know any of these?" Hawk said.

Tony looked at the list.

"Don't see no brothers on this list," Tony said.

"Anybody you know?" Hawk said.

"Man, they all got those fucking bohunk do-do names, you know? I can't tell one from another one."

"Well, me and Spenser gonna be prowling around some of your neighborhoods," Hawk said. "You got any problem with that?"

"Live and let live." Tony sat.

"I think he means it's okay," I said to Hawk.

"We be prowling either way," Hawk said.

Tony smiled.

"You want a drink?" he said. "On the house. People see whitey at the bar, justify the new name."

"Like to help you out," I said. "But it's a little early."

"Whoa," Tony said. "I remember the days when you'd drink paint remover at nine in the morning."

"Never drank paint remover," I said.

"And we proud of you for that," Hawk said.

"Drop in anytime," Tony said.

"Anything helpful," Hawk said to him, "you know where to find me."

"Harbor Health Club. Leave a message with Henry."

"Nice to be remembered," Hawk said.

"Nothing to do with you," Tony said. "I don't forget much."

Hawk stood. I stood with him. Tony stayed seated. Nobody shook hands.

"Good luck," Tony said.

"Got nothing to do with luck," Hawk said.

12

———•———

"WHAT DO YOU THINK of Tony's story?" I said.

Hawk and I were sitting at the counter, having lunch, at the Town Diner in Watertown.

"Well," Hawk said. "Bunch of white guys with funny names come pushing into Tony's territory, and Tony lets it slide."

"Because he was mad at Gillespie?" I said. "And a couple of others?"

"And because some of the people the white guys with funny names rousted didn't belong to Tony?"

"There is no black crime in Boston that doesn't belong to Tony," I said.

"How long you think Luther Gillespie last, he starts skimming on Tony?"

"Not as long as he did," I said. "Are you saying that Tony's story doesn't ring true."

"I'm saying it's bullshit."

"Maybe Tony's afraid of the Ukes," I said.

"He ain't even afraid of you and me," Hawk said.

"He is intrepid," I said.

Hawk took a bite of his BLT and nodded while he chewed.

"Something else going on," Hawk said when he'd swallowed.

"Maybe they're cutting him in?" I said.

"On what," Hawk said. "It's all his anyway. Why he willing to share it?"

"We've ruled out fear," I said.

Hawk nodded.

"Tony ain't afraid," Hawk said.

"And we've ruled out inattention."

"What's the last thing you can think of, Tony didn't notice?"

I was having apple pie for lunch. With cheese. I ate some and drank some coffee. Hawk was drinking orange juice. He asked for another glass.

"Okay, we've ruled out inattention," I said.

"How 'bout love?"

Hawk smiled.

"Okay, no love," I said. "That leaves greed."

Hawk patted his mouth with his napkin.

"It does."

"But not just a cut of what he's already got," I said.

"He keeps what he's got," Hawk said. "And he gets what somebody else got."

"That would be Tony," I said. "So how does that work with the Ukrainians?"

"Maybe Tony playing them."

"Maybe they're playing him."

"Likely they playing each other," Hawk said.

"Likely," I said.

We were quiet while we finished lunch. I had some more coffee. Hawk ate only half of his sandwich. I looked at it.

"No good?" I said.

"Excellent," Hawk said. "Just don't eat so much anymore."

"Because they shot up your alimentary canal?" I said.

"Something like that," Hawk said. "Like orange juice though."

"Maybe you could write a diet book," I said.

"The sniper diet?"

"I could help you with the writing," I said, "being as I'm white and all."

"We get to that, massa," Hawk said, "soon as we clean up the Ukrainians."

"Be nice if we knew the connection."

"Would be," Hawk said.

"Got a guess?"

"No."

"What the hell is in it for Tony," I said.

"Money," Hawk said.

13

———•———

I HAD SHOWERED and shaved and brushed my teeth and put on my new black silk boxers. I was sitting on the couch in Susan's living room with my feet on a russet-colored leather hassock, reading the *Sunday Globe* while Pearl lay beside me with her feet in the air. Susan came into the living room, fresh from her bath, wearing a short blue kimono, and flashed me.

"Am I to understand that it's time?" I said.

"You are," she said.

"Have you thought of any way to keep Pearl from yowling at the door when we go into the bedroom and close it?"

"No."

"But we're not going to leave the door open," I said.

"Not unless you want a ménage à trois," Susan said.

"Well," I said. "I guess we can put up with it."

"Maybe we can think of something to do," Susan said, "to keep our minds off it."

I followed her down to her bedroom. We closed the door. In a moment we heard Pearl's footsteps. Then silence. Then a scratch at the door. We got into bed together. Pearl began to cry at the door. Susan rolled over and kissed me. I kissed her back. In a little while I was hardly aware of Pearl. After a time, when Susan had let go of me and my breathing had returned to normal, I got up and let Pearl in.

She dashed into the room, jumped on the bed, turned around about twelve times, and plumped down hard against Susan, in the spot that until recently had been occupied by me. In the process, she scrambled the covers so that Susan had none and was lying naked on the bed. We'd been naked in each other's presence quite often. Yet Susan always had a quality of unease about her when she was naked, as if she'd been caught doing something embarrassing. I found the quality endearing. Pearl put her head on Susan's stomach and stared at me. I stared at her. Susan couldn't reach the covers without dislodging Pearl. She looked uneasy. Pearl didn't move.

"I think I'll start breakfast," I said.

"Fine," Susan said.

I didn't move. Pearl didn't move. Susan looked uneasy. Then she smiled.

"You're dying," she said, "aren't you? To say something about a dog and a pussy."

"Not in Cambridge," I said, and began to put on my pants.

Most Sundays, since we normally got a late start, we spent nearly half the daylight hours sitting in Susan's kitchen, having breakfast together. Susan set the table and I cooked. This morning I was cooking scrapple and eggs when Susan came into the kitchen, dressed in pale pink sweats with her hair in place and makeup perfectly on. Pearl remained at least for the moment on Susan's bed, apparently intent on fully reclaiming it. Susan poured herself some orange juice and sipped it as she set the table.

"What is in scrapple?" she said.

"Cornmeal and pig parts," I said.

Susan put her orange juice down while she fluffed up some flowers in a vase on the table.

"How enticing," Susan said.

"It's worse than it sounds," I said.

"I'm sure it will be lovely," Susan said. "Did you learn anything from Tony Marcus?"

"We suspect that Tony is not being entirely forthright."

"I'm shocked," Susan said.

I told her about Tony. Susan listened to me with full-faced attention. She didn't interrupt. She never interrupted if the discussion was other than playful.

"You're saying that Tony Marcus could drive these people out," she said when I finished, "if he chose to."

"Yes," I said. "These are tough guys. But they're in Tony's neighborhood, surrounded by Tony's people, and he's got them outnumbered."

"So he gets something out of having them there."

"Money."

"You're sure?"

"No, but what else does Tony care about?"

"Maybe nothing," Susan said. "But if it's true, he is unusual."

"Might be worthwhile to keep the question open," I said.

"I'm not advocating anything," Susan said. "But what difference does it make? Hawk knows the four men. Why not find them and kill them."

"Hawk hasn't said."

"And you have no theory?"

"Well, maybe a small one," I said.

I put the scrapple slices on a platter with the fried eggs and poured the coffee and sat down.

"My guess is that Hawk intends to get the whole Ukrainian thing out of the black community."

"Does he care that much about the community?"

"No. Hawk has no community. I think his pride has taken a huge hit, and he has to do that to rectify his pride."

"Defeat them totally," Susan said.

I nodded.

"So the four men are not enough," she said.

"No."

She nodded to herself quietly.

"So he has to be sure who actually did what," she said. "And he has to know everything and everyone in the—what shall we call it—Ukrainian conspiracy?"

"Yes."

"And you are to help him."

"I will help him."

Susan concentrated on stirring Equal into her coffee.

"The two of you are going to root out a whole ethnic criminal enterprise," she said.

"I think that's the plan," I said.

She stirred some more.

"That sounds daunting."

"It certainly does," I said.

Susan was looking at the small, circular movement she had stirred up in her coffee cup. Then she looked up at me with the full force of herself. The force was almost physical.

"On the other hand," she said, "if the Ukrainians knew the both of you as I do, they might find it a little daunting themselves."

"I hope so," I said.

14

———•———

THE LAW FIRM of Duda and Husak was on the tenth floor of an office building on Boylston Street near Tremont. We parked in the garage at the Millennium Center and walked back. The lobby of the old building was narrow and trimmed with tarnished gilt. The gray marble floor was cracked and faded. The elevator was a mesh cage. It rose as though it had lost all interest years ago. It eased to a clumsy stop on the tenth floor. We walked down another narrow corridor with a worn marble floor. The marble was cracked and faded, and the once even marble threshold to Duda and Husak dipped in the center, rounded with use.

A nasty-looking gray-haired woman with a hint of facial hair sat in an armless swivel chair behind an old conference table, reading the *Boston Herald.* The table held a phone and a computer and not much else. She looked at us with contempt. Probably most of the clients that sought the services of Duda and Husak were contemptible. Not us.

"Can I help you?" she said.

"We here to see either Duda or Husak," Hawk said. "Don't matter which."

"Mr. Duda is not in," she said.

There were two doors on the other side of the secretary. One of the doors was open, and we could see a man at the desk with his coat off, talking on the phone. The other door was closed.

"Then we'll see Mr. Husak," Hawk said.

We walked toward the open door.

"Hey," she said.

We ignored her and went on into the office. She followed us in, saying, "Hey, hey, hey."

Husak said "Hold on" into the phone and looked at us.

"What's going on?" he said.

"We come to talk Ukrainians," Hawk said.

Husak said, "Then maybe you should have made an appointment."

Hawk sat in one of the client chairs. The office was small and no better looking than the rest of the building. It smelled of desperation accumulated over years. Behind Husak's desk was a dirty window that overlooked an air shaft.

Hawk looked at the secretary.

"You can go now, missy," he said.

"I ain't no missy," she said, and looked at Husak.

He nodded. And she went out. I closed the door behind her. Then I sat. He spoke into the phone again.

"Got a coupla guys here I need to listen to," he said. "I'll buzz you back in a while."

He hung up and tipped his chair back and put his feet up.

"So whadya need in such a hurry?" he said.

"Name of the people hired you to represent Bohdan Dziubakevych," Hawk said.

"Who?"

"Bohdan Dziubakevych," Hawk said.

I was impressed.

"Never heard of him," Husak said. "Who the hell are you?"

"Me and my faithful honkie be members of the Ukrainian Royal Family."

"What the fuck are you talking about?" Husak said. "I got shit to do. I got no time to be flapping my gums with you."

Hawk stood and walked past Husak and opened the window behind him.

"What are you doing?" Husak said. "It's fucking freezing out."

"It is," Hawk said. "Isn't it."

He took hold of Husak's hair and yanked him out of his chair and spun him around. He shifted his grip to the back of Husak's shirt and the crotch of Husak's pants and picked him up and stuck him headfirst halfway out the window. Husak began to scream—short screams, one coming right after another, quietly so as not to make Hawk lose his grip. His body was rigid, but he didn't dare struggle. In slow desperation, he reached carefully back, trying to find something to hold on to. Hawk shook him a little, as if he were dusty.

"I don't like you," Hawk said to him in a reasonable voice. "I got no reason not to let you go unless you got something you can tell me that I might want to hear."

Husak kept up the short soft screaming. Hawk brought him in and held him with Husak's head still out the window and his chest resting on the sill. Husak's short screams morphed into gasping.

"Royal Ukrainians don't fuck around," Hawk said calmly. "Who hired you to represent Bohdan?"

Husak kept gasping.

"You go out again," Hawk said. "I let go."

"Boots," Husak gasped.

The pulse in his neck was beating visibly.

"Boots who?" Hawk said.

"Boots Podolak," Husak said.

Hawk looked at me. I nodded. Hawk pulled Husak off the window and stood him up and sat him in his chair. He left the window open. Husak sat rigid in the chair. His face was pale. He was trembling.

"He hire both of you?" Hawk said.

"Not him personally, but a guy said he was from him," Husak said. His voice was hoarse, but the gasping had slowed. "Paid us in cash. Up front. Me and Duda both."

"He want you to give them the best defense you could?" Hawk said.

"He wanted to make sure Bohdan didn't roll over."

Husak was limp. There was no snap left in him. He was eager to answer questions. The only danger in someone like that was that he'd figure out what you wanted to hear and tell you that. Tell you anything. Ten stories is a long way down. The unpleasant secretary knocked on the office door.

"Mr. Husak? Is everything all right."

"Tell her yes," Hawk said gently.

Husak raised his voice.

"Fine, Nancy, everything's fine."

"You the one told Bohdan not to testify?" Hawk said.

"No . . ."

Hawk glanced at the window.

"I did," Husak said. "We both did. Bohdan had family back in Ukraine. If he testified, they were all going to be killed."

"You told him that."

"Yes."

"He believed you."

"Yes," Husak said. "I showed him a finger with a wedding ring on it."

"A finger?" I said.

"Yes. It was his mother's. He recognized the ring."

"Somebody cut off his mother's finger and sent it to you?"

"Yes. It was neat. Wrapped in plastic, you know?"

"And you showed it to Bohdan," I said.

"Yeah."

"He know they were going to kill him in prison?" Hawk said.

"No, I don't think so."

"You arrange that?"

"No," Husak said. "Honest to God I didn't. I just, I just told Boots when I was going to visit Bohdan."

"You represent the other four?" Hawk said.

"Me and Duda," Husak said.

"Tell me about them."

"They never said a word to me," Husak said. "I don't know if they speak English. Whatever I said to them, the four of them would just look at me without any expression, like I was a . . ." he rolled his hands as he searched for the word. "Like I wasn't anything. Duda speaks a little Ukrainian. He did what talking there was."

"What did he say?" Hawk asked.

"He said they expected to be acquitted. He said we should do what Boots said for us to do."

"That's all."

"That's all, I swear on my mother, I don't know anything else. I promise."

"Where's Duda," Hawk said.

"He's in Miami. Took a week off. He'll be back next week."

"When he get back," Hawk said, "I want to see him. Have him call my faithful ofay."

I took a business card out and put it on Husak's desk.

"He call me and we all have a civilized discussion. He don't call me, you go out the window, and so does he."

"Yeah. He'll call. Honest to God he'll call, I know he will."

Hawk went around the desk and closed the window. Husak's face pinched and unpinched.

"Don't tell anyone it was me that talked," Husak said.

Hawk nodded as though his mind was elsewhere.

"You have no idea what these people are like. They aren't like other people. They find out I talked to you, they'll chop me up into pieces."

"Who'll do the chopping," Hawk said.

"Some Ukrainian," Husak said. "They're like from the fucking Stone Age, you know? I wish I never seen any of them."

"I find out you're lying to me," Hawk said, "I'll make sure they know you was talking."

"Everything I told you is the truth, so help me God."

"The whole truth?" Hawk said.

"So help me God," Husak said.

Hawk looked at me.

"Got a nice legal sound, don't it," Hawk said.

15

WE WALKED ALONG Boylston Street toward the new parking garage in Millennium Place. Traffic had become so desperate in Boston during the Big Dig that even the good hydrants were taken.

"Would you have dropped him?" I said.

"Don't have to decide now," Hawk said. "Who's Boots Podolak?"

"The mayor of Marshport," I said.

"Didn't know they had a mayor," Hawk said.

"City of eighty thousand," I said.

"Knew it was big enough," Hawk said. "Didn't know it was civilized."

"Boots isn't much of a civilizing influence," I said. "Mayor is just the official title. Actually, he's the owner."

"Eighty thousand," Hawk said.

"Yep."

"How many white?"

"Boots and his management team," I said. "And a small immigrant Ukrainian population."

"Rest of the plantation?"

"African and Hispanic," I said.

"How Boots pull that off?" Hawk said.

"Marshport used to be mostly middle European. Boots is a holdover."

"What kind of name is that?" Hawk said. "Marshport?"

He flattened the *a* and dropped the *r*'s in parody of the local accent.

I said, "Named after some prominent family, I think."

"Why you suppose Boots hiring lawyers for Ukrainians?" Hawk said.

"Podolak might be Ukrainian," I said.

"Or Polish," Hawk said.

"Didn't parts of Ukraine used to be Polish?" I said. "Or vice versa?"

"You asking me?" Hawk said. "You the one sleeping with a Harvard grad."

"And Cecile?" I said.

"The med school," Hawk said. "They just know 'bout corpuscles and shit. Susan got a damn Ph.D."

"You seen Cecile lately?" I said.

"Yes," Hawk said.

We were waiting now for the elevator down to our parking level. There were things you pressed Hawk on, and things you didn't. They didn't belong to categories. One had to sense subtleties of tone and posture to know which was which. Cecile was a no press.

"Maybe Boots is in on it with the Ukrainians," I said. "Moving in on Tony."

"Expand the plantation?" Hawk said.

I shrugged.

"Think it be more like the other way around, wouldn't you," Hawk said.

"Tony moving in on a black city?"

"Un-huh."

"You would think that," I said.

"'Cept far as we can tell it ain't so."

"Far as we can tell," I said.

"You know Boots?" Hawk said when we were in his car.

"Yes."

"He remember you?"

"He would," I said.

"Fondly?" Hawk said.

"No," I said.

"You know where we can find him?" Hawk said.

"Yep."

"Then let's go see him."

"Okay," I said.

Hawk pulled onto the last block of Boylston Street.

"Think we can get there from here?"

"Just barely," I said.

16

———•———

MARSHPORT CITY HALL was one of those handsome, ornate civic buildings that people built in the nineteenth century out of brownstone and brick. It had the affluent, satisfied look of the upper middle class it was built for and was probably the best-looking thing in the city . . . except for me and Hawk, and we were only temporary. Inside was a lot of curving staircase, and dark wood, and heavy oil paintings of the city's ancestry, who for all I knew could have been the entire Marsh dynasty. The mayor's office was on the second floor, facing the big stairwell. We went in and announced to the several blue-haired staff ladies that we wanted to see the mayor. I gave my name. Hawk smiled warmly, which seemed to fluster the closest staff member a little.

She got up and went into the mayor's office and came out shortly with Boots Podolak behind her.

"Spenser," he said loudly, "you son of a bitch."

"Nice to be remembered, Boots."

"You still on the cops?"

"Nope. Private now."

"Then get the fuck out of my building," Podolak said.

He looked at Hawk.

"And take Sambo the fuck with you."

"Sambo," Hawk said to me.

The blue-haired staff pretended he hadn't said that. All of them appeared to have typing to do.

"We've come to discuss Duda and Husak," I said. "Esquire."

"I think they both Esquire," Hawk said.

"You think I should have said Esquires?"

"I dunno," Hawk said.

He looked at Podolak.

"You think, does one Esquire cover both lawyers?" Hawk said to Podolak.

"What the fuck are you talking about."

"Your attorneys," I said. "Duda and Husak."

Podolak was a tall, bony man with a sparse gray crew cut,

and a thin gray 1930s movie villain moustache. He wore rimless glasses, and his arms were long. He was narrow and hard-looking. He wore no coat, and under his tan cardigan sweater an incongruous potbelly pressed out, as if he was hiding a soccer ball.

"In the office," he said, and stepped aside so Hawk and I could walk through the door. Podolak shut the door behind us and walked the length of the vast office and sat behind a vast desk. There were four other men sitting around at the near end of the office. Podolak didn't say anything to them, nor did he introduce anyone. He took a long, thin cigar from a leather humidor and got it lit, turning it slowly in the flame of a pigskin-covered desk lighter. Hawk and I sat in a couple of chairs near his desk and watched the operation. When he was happy with the way it was burning, Boots looked at us through the cigar smoke.

"So what's this shit about Duda-dooda?" he said.

"You hired him and Husak to represent some Ukrainians with names I can't pronounce," Hawk said. "If I could remember them. And you tell them, make sure nobody rolls on nobody."

"You think so, huh."

"We do," Hawk said. "And we want to know why."

Boots puffed his cigar for a moment, looking at Hawk, then at me.

"Where'd you get him?" Boots said to me.

"Bought him from a guy in Louisiana," I said. "Then came emancipation and I'm stuck with him."

If Boots thought I was funny, he didn't show it. Which happens to me a lot.

"So who told you I hired Duda and whatsis?" Boots said.

The four men in the far corner of the room had stood up and were watching us.

"Whatsis," Hawk said.

"Well, he's full of shit, whoever he is. I need a lawyer, I don't need to go into Boston."

"Why you think they from Boston?" Hawk said.

Boots pulled on his cigar for a moment. Then he took it out and admired it. Then he looked straight at Hawk.

"What I don't need," he said, "is some smart-ass fucking nigger coming in here and talking to me like he's white."

Hawk smiled at him warmly.

"Ah know," he said. "Ah know . . . and yet, here ah is. You got something going with Tony Marcus?"

"Who the fuck is Tony Marcus?" Boots said.

Hawk made a dismissive gesture with his hand.

"Lemme ask you this," Hawk said. "You don't know anybody named Duda and Husak. You don't know nobody named Tony Marcus. You don't want us here. You the mayor. You got four, ah, retainers standing around down the other end of the room, lookin' terrifying. Whyn't you just throw us out?"

"These men are Marshport police officers," Podolak said with dignity.

"Oh, good," Hawk said. "I was afraid for a minute they be real cops."

"You want to go to jail?" Podolak said.

Hawk looked at me. Then he looked down the room at the four men. Then he looked at Podolak, and stood and walked down the room and stopped in front of the four men, standing very close to them.

"I don't think so," he said.

No one moved. The air in the room seemed to thicken. I could feel the pressure of it.

Looking at the four men, Hawk was still talking to Boots.

"You let us in here," he said, "'cause you hoping to find out what we knew 'bout you hiring Duda and Husak. And then I say something 'bout Tony Marcus and you want to know what we know 'bout him."

Nobody moved. Podolak and the four cops were giving Hawk the steely stare, and he was, I thought, bearing up very well under it. Hawk kept looking at the four cops as he talked to Podolak.

"Tha's one reason you ain't thrown us out," Hawk said.

"What's the other reason?" Podolak said.

He was trying to look at ease and in control. I thought he was struggling with it a little.

"Other reason bein'," Hawk said, "that there only five of

you and there two of us, which means we got you outnumbered."

The cop closest to Hawk was a big, shambling guy with grayish hair and a lot of broken veins in his face.

"Enough," he said.

He took a leather sap out of his right hip pocket, and put a big left hand flat on Hawk's chest. Hawk smiled at him. And then something happened and Hawk had the sap and the cop was on the floor with blood running from his nose. I had my gun in my hand. For the occasion I had shelved the usual S&W .38. I was carrying my Browning nine-millimeter, which I pointed at the cops.

"Okay," I said. "Everybody sit tight."

Podolak was outraged.

"You can't shoot up the fucking mayor's office, for crissake," he said.

The office door opened and one of the blue-haired secretaries peered in.

She said, "Is there anything you need, Mr. Mayor?"

Hawk walked back toward Podolak, slapping the sap lightly against his thigh. When he reached the desk he looked at Podolak for a moment. Then he tossed the sap on Podolak's desk and with a very fast, fluid motion produced a big .44 Mag from inside his coat.

The secretary said, "Oh my God," and backed out the door and closed it.

Hawk didn't even glance at her. He cocked the revolver.

The noise of the hammer going back was loud in the brittle silence. Then a loud alarm horn began to blare from somewhere in City Hall. If Hawk heard it, he showed no sign.

"Gimme something I can use," Hawk said.

He pressed the barrel of the cocked revolver against the bridge of Podolak's nose.

"Now," Hawk said.

The three cops left standing shuffled a little. But nobody made any decisive movements. Podolak's body was rigid. His face looked moist. And quite pale. His throat moved as he swallowed.

"Quick," Hawk said.

"Ask Tony about his daughter," Podolak said.

Hawk smiled and nodded. With the gun still pressed against the bridge of Podolak's nose, he let the hammer down slowly on the .44. Podolak let out a little sound. Hawk nodded his head at me and went to the door, carrying the .44 comfortably by his side, the barrel pointing at the floor. I backed toward the door after him.

"Door's open," Hawk said.

I backed through it. Hawk closed it and grinned at me, and we both sprinted out of the mayor's office, which had been deserted by the blue-haired staff, down the grand staircase where a number of City Hall staffers mingled in uncertain anxiety, and out the front door. I could hear a siren sounding somewhere. As we rounded the corner, I spotted a police car pulling up in front of City Hall. Then we were in Hawk's car and rolling.

There was very little traffic in the desolate city. What there was was outbound, like us. Maybe nobody drove into Marshport. We headed back to Boston on 1A without hearing any more of the siren. And without seeing a cop.

I said to Hawk, "I don't sense hot pursuit."

"Probably didn't chase us," Hawk said.

"Because?"

"They afraid they might catch us," Hawk said.

17

THE FOUR UKRAINIANS all had the same address in a ratty duplex off Market Street in a neighborhood that was downscale even for Marshport. The house was rented to Vanko Tsyklins'kyj. Hawk and I sat in the car for a while and looked at it.

"Podolak'll never think of looking for us here," I said.

Hawk didn't answer. He stared at the house.

"Lower half of the windows," Hawk said, "boarded up."

I nodded.

"Cellar windows are entirely covered."

Hawk nodded.

"Lets go ring the bell," he said.

We got out of the car and walked toward the house. I was wearing my Smith & Wesson .38, butt forward, on the left side of my belt, and carrying a Browning nine-millimeter, with a round in the chamber on my right hip. I felt like Wild Bill Hickok. Nothing moved in the house that we could see as we walked across the street. The front door had a peephole. Hawk rang the bell. After a moment, the door opened two inches on a security bolt. A face appeared in the opening. The face didn't speak.

"Vanko," Hawk said.

"Not home."

"You're Vanko," Hawk said.

"Not home."

"You speak English?" Hawk said.

"No."

Hawk looked at the face for a time.

"It's not over, Vanko," Hawk said. "It's just starting."

The face didn't show any reaction. Nor did it move. Hawk turned and walked away. I followed him. I heard the door close behind us. My back felt as if someone had painted a bull's-eye on it. We got in Hawk's car and sat some more.

"Door's metal," I said.

"Yes."

"We can sit," I said. "They have to come out sometime."

Hawk shook his head.

"I done what I wanted to do," he said.

"They know you're back," I said.

"Un-huh."

"Which means they'll probably feel obligated to have another run at you."

"Wouldn't you?" Hawk said. "I come calling?"

"Especially if I was really successful the first time."

"Thanks for remembering," Hawk said.

"I still think Vinnie might be helpful here," I said.

"Don't need no help," Hawk said.

He was looking steadily at the house.

"No," I said. "Of course not. But I do. Ukrainians might be colorblind and shoot me instead."

"Un-huh."

"He'd be protecting me," I said.

Hawk shrugged. He was still looking at the house. A few snowflakes began to skitter aimlessly.

"Long as he ain't protecting them," Hawk said.

18

THE LAST SNOWFALL of the season had started. The first serious snowflakes were falling purposefully down, past my office window onto Berkeley Street. The city seemed to hunch up a little and hurry a little, getting ready. I decided not to turn on the office television. As I matured, my taste for manufactured hysteria was beginning to decline. It was late winter. In late winter, it snowed in Boston. Sometimes it snowed in early spring. I had lived here all my adult life. I was starting to get used to it.

Cecile came into my office, wearing a very incorrect fur coat, a few hints of melted snow gleaming in her thick, black hair. I stood and took her coat.

"A lot of beaver died for this coat," I said.

"Be very careful with the beaver remarks," Cecile said with a smile. "Besides, it's mink. And the little darlings died during orgasm."

"What better way," I said.

Cecile sat in a chair in front of my desk and crossed her splendid legs. She was wearing high-heeled leather boots, which would be almost as good as bare feet in a snowfall. I offered coffee. She accepted. I got it for her and some for myself. Who cares about sleeping. Then I sat behind my desk and admired her knees.

"Are you looking at my legs?" Cecile said.

"I am," I said. "I'm a firm believer in racial equality."

"And sexism," Cecile said.

"In its place," I said.

Cecile smiled.

"Hawk and I are seeing one another again," she said.

"Good," I said.

"How do you think he is?"

"Fine," I said.

"He seems just the same to me," she said.

"Yes," I said.

"But he shouldn't be," Cecile said.

"Because?"

"Because he was badly hurt, almost killed, and, what to call it, professionally compromised, I guess."

"Stuff happens," I said.

"But there's no sign that it affected him."

"It affected him," I said.

"And how would you know that?"

"It would affect me," I said.

"And you're just like him?"

"No one's just like Hawk," I said. "But I'm less unlike him than many."

"And you wouldn't have a moment or two of—*why me?*"

"You can't do what I do, let alone what Hawk does, and go around saying why me? You're a surgeon. You must know about dying."

Cecile nodded.

"What was it like for you?" she said.

"Well, the thing about almost dying," I said, "is that a lot of the time, you don't know that you almost died until a long time after you didn't. When Hawk came into the hospital, he was unconscious. He was in surgery for something like twelve hours. And in intensive care something like ten days. Most of that time he was unaware."

"Intensive care can be a very brutal experience," Cecile said.

"It is," I said. "But most of the time you don't know it. You wake up for a moment and something awful is going on that you'd rather not remember and then you're gone again. And even after you start being awake, you're so whacko that it's aimless to evaluate anything you might be thinking. I thought there were dioramas in the overhead lights."

"The nurses call it ICU syndrome," Cecile said. "Trauma, extended anesthesia, painkillers, sleep deprivation . . ." she waved her hand.

"I was paranoid delusional," I said, "even after I got out of ICU. I pulled all the hookups out one night, because I thought I was escaping something. Paul Giacomon was in from Chicago, and after that, he and Hawk and Susan took turns spending the night with me. They were the only ones I trusted not to be in on the conspiracy."

"Did you know you were crazy?"

"I did, I knew I was in the hospital. And I knew I was in a freezing cold railroad station in New Bedford, being stalked by somebody."

"Both realities equally," Cecile said.

"And simultaneously."

"So by the time you are awake and rational," she said, "you are pretty much out of danger. In effect, though you've had a miserable time, you did not experience *almost dying*. You only heard about it afterwards."

"That's exactly right," I said.

"Do you think that's Hawk's experience?"

"Yes."

"Have you talked about it with him?"

"No."

"And the weakness?" she said. "The dependence?"

"Don't they teach you this stuff in med school?" I said.

Cecile smiled.

"There might have been something one semester," she said, "sophomore year. It was an eight o'clock class, and it wasn't crucial, you know, like suturing, so a lot of us probably rested."

"You feel like shit for a long time. And if you're a big, strong, tough guy like Hawk, you're not used to it, and you hate it. And you hate being hooked up to the hat rack, and you hate that you can't walk to the bathroom alone. But you know that will pass. You know you'll get it back. All it takes is patience and work. And you know you can wait and you know you can work. So you know, in a while, you'll be what you were."

"So you shut up about it," Cecile said. "And do what you can and wait."

"I recall that I whined some to Susan," I said.

"And when you got well enough you put the matter right," Cecile said.

"Hawk and I."

"And then you were whole."

"Something like that."

"And that's what you and he are doing now," Cecile said.

"Yes."

Outside my office window the snow was coming fast now,

swirling a little as the wind eddied down Berkeley Street. We both looked at it quietly for a while.

"He's never talked to me about this."

I nodded.

"Have you ever talked to Susan about this?"

"Yes."

"Why can't he talk to me about these things? For Christ's sake, I'm even a damned doctor."

"It's not a medical matter," I said. "My identity, if I may be permitted the tired phrase, is me and Susan. Hawk's is still Hawk."

"You're saying he doesn't love me."

"No. If I thought he didn't love you, I'd have said, 'He doesn't love you.' We talked about this before. Hawk and I grew up different. I grew up in Laramie, Wyoming, in a house where my father and my two uncles loved me and looked out for me. Hawk grew up on the streets in a ghetto, and for a long time he looked out for himself, until Bobby Nevins found him when Hawk was fifteen. He ever tell you about Bobby Nevins?"

"No."

"Ask him to. It's interesting."

"Are you actually explaining the black experience to me?" Cecile said.

"I'm explaining Hawk. Nevins trained him, but no one, as far as I know, ever loved him. Hawk is what he is because he has found a way to be faithful to what he is, since he was a kid."

"I love him," Cecile said.

"For him, that's a learning experience."

"And he won't change," Cecile said.

"If he changed he might cease to exist," I said. "He's with you now."

"Not all of him."

"Probably not."

"Do you think I'll ever have all of him?"

"Maybe not," I said.

"And if I want to be with him, I have to accept that possibility," Cecile said.

I smiled at her as encouragingly as I could and nodded my head. The snow was coming so hard now that it was difficult to see the FAO Schwarz store across the street.

"Yes," I said. "You do."

19

HAWK AND I SAT with a State Police captain named Healy in his office at 1010 Commonwealth, talking about Marshport.

"Bohunks run it since the Pilgrims," Healy said. "Then after the war it began to shift. All that's left is one Ukrainian neighborhood, where Boots is from. The rest is mostly black, mostly Caribbean black. We think of them all as Hispanic. Or black. But they don't. They think they're Puerto Rican, Jamaican, Haitian, Costa Rican, Dominican, Guatemalan."

"So even though they a majority, they don't have think so because they don't think they all the same."

Healy nodded.

"So the Bohunks still in charge," Hawk said.

"It's more specific than that," Healy said. "Boots Podolak is in charge."

"Tell us about Boots," I said.

"Boots's grandfather took Marshport away from the Yankees," Healy said. "And his father inherited it and passed it on to Boots."

"They control it."

"Completely," Healy said. "Cops, firemen, probation officers, district court judges, aldermen, state reps, congressmen, school superintendents, restaurant owners, car dealers, liquor distributors, junk dealers, dope, whores, numbers . . ." Healy spread his hands. "Everything."

"And you can't close him down."

"I can't because I'm the homicide commander and it ain't my job," Healy said. "But it's a closed corporation and nobody will talk. Witnesses die. Informants disappear. Undercover cops disappear. Judges get intimidated."

Healy's office was on the top floor, and through the window behind his desk I could see the snow still falling evenly, and the plows lunging fitfully along Commonwealth Avenue, trying to stay ahead of it.

"You met Boots?" Healy said.

"Yes," Hawk said.

"You?" Healy said to me.

"Yes."

"At the same time?" Healy said. "Both of you?"

"Yes," I said.

Healy smiled.

"That must have been interesting."

"How big an operation is Boots running," Hawk said.

"About eighty thousand," Healy said.

"The whole city."

"Yep."

"How many people with guns."

Healy thought about it.

"Lemme make a call," he said.

"Maybe you don't have to," Hawk said. "Does he have as many shooters as Tony Marcus?"

"Oh, hell, yes."

"As good?"

"Hell, yes. He's got some Ukrainians would kill you for eating a Tootsie Roll," Healy said, "then take it out of your dead mouth and finish it."

"These homegrown Ukrainians," Hawk said. "Or Ukrainian Ukrainians."

"Imported," Healy said.

"How 'bout Boots?" I said.

"Don't look like much," Healy said, "does he?"

"He stands his ground pretty good," I said.

"Does he?" Healy said.

I shrugged. Hawk looked impassive, which is one of Hawk's best things.

"Ain't it great," Healy said, "how those of us in and out of law enforcement can share information in the common good."

"He looks like a mean funeral director," I said.

"He's a psychopath," Healy said. "Or is it sociopath. I can't keep it straight."

"He's a whack job," I said.

"He is," Healy said. "He's not such a whack job that he can't see what's in his best interest, and he's not such a whack job that he can't do what's in his best interest. He can take care of business. But if it's good for business, he'll do anything. Kill, torture, maim, chop up small children, whatever. A lot of people have died lousy deaths because of him."

Healy looked at Hawk.

"You think you were almost one of them?" he said.

Hawk shrugged.

"I'll know, sooner or later," he said.

"As a police officer, of course it is my obligation," Healy said, "to warn you against taking the law into your own hands."

I said, "Of course, captain."

"Still," Healy said, "'twould be a darlin' thing if the rat bastard were dead."

"Darlin'," I said.

"You Mickeys do talk strange," Hawk said. "You know any connection between Boots and Tony Marcus?"

"No," Healy said. "I can check with the Organized Crime Unit. Give you a call."

"Thanks." Hawk said. "Call Spenser."

Healy grinned.

"Wouldn't want me knowing how to find you, would we," he said.

"We would not," Hawk said.

20

WE WERE IN Hawk's snow car, a Lincoln Navigator. The wipers worked steadily. The snow was unflinching.

"A Navy pilot ever land on this thing?" I said. "By mistake?"

"I try not to drive it near the coast," Hawk said. "You know Tony had a daughter?"

"No," I said.

"Who would know 'bout that?" Hawk said.

"Nobody I can think of," I said.

"Guess we gonna have to ask Tony."

"Maybe Boots was blowing smoke," I said, "so you wouldn't shoot him."

"No," Hawk said. "I was looking in his eyes. He was telling me as little as he could. But he weren't lying."

"He won't like that we dissed him in his own office," I said.

"Diss him where we find him," Hawk said. "Lotta people ain't going to like us, 'fore we're through."

"Probably including Tony," I said.

"Probably."

"We could start handing out numbers," I said. "Like a deli."

There was a snow emergency parking ban, so Hawk dropped the four wheel drive into low range, pulled the Navigator into the alley behind my office, jammed it up onto the sidewalk by the back entrance to my building, and parked. We went up the back stairs to my office.

We hung up our coats. I made some coffee. While I was doing that, Hawk stood in the window bay and watched it snow. I got some cream out of the office refrigerator, and sugar from the office-supply cabinet. I put out two thick white china mugs, and the cream and sugar, on my desk. I went to the closet, unlocked it, and got a bottle of "Black Bush" Irish whisky from the shelf and set it down beside the mugs.

"Snow emergency," I said.

"You gonna need another mug," Hawk said.

"Who?"

"Captain Martin Quirk," Hawk said. "His driver just let

him out on the corner and is now parked there, screwing up the traffic."

"He feeling bad about that?" I said.

"I only guessing," Hawk said. "But I say no."

I went and got some spoons and a third mug. Susan had bought me the mugs from a restaurant supply catalogue. She said they were the perfect masculine complement to my Mr. Coffee machine. She might have been needling me. I had just put the spoons down and the extra mug beside the other two when Quirk came in. He was wearing a dark gray tweed overcoat with raglan sleeves, his collar turned up. He wore no hat, and his hair was flecked with still-unmelted snow.

Quirk looked at the mugs and the bottle.

"That looks encouraging," he said.

"You off duty?" I said.

"On my way home," Quirk said.

I poured coffee into the mugs, added sugar and cream to mine and a significant slosh of whisky, and set the bottle out for the others.

"Hawk tells me your driver is impeding traffic," I said.

"Christ, there's got to be some fun being a cop," Quirk said.

All three of us sipped our enhanced coffee for a moment. The storm wasn't one of those raging ones. It was a placid, persistent storm. Not too much wind. Not too brutally cold. Merely the implacable quiet snowfall outside the window.

Quirk set his coffee mug down on the edge of my desk

and hung his coat on the rack, and sat down near his coffee. Hawk continued to watch the snow fall.

"You're looking strong, Hawk," Quirk said.

"I am," Hawk said.

"Probably get in trouble if you quoted me," Quirk said, "but I'm glad to hear it."

"Won't never tell," Hawk said.

"You boys recall the law firm of Duda and Husak," Quirk said.

"They represented Bohdan and the Ukrainians," I said.

"Sounds like a band my daughter listens to," Quirk said. "Yeah, them."

He drank some more coffee and tilted the chair back a little so that the front feet were off the ground.

"Went to see them just the other day," Hawk said.

"I knew that," Quirk said.

He rocked his chair slightly, keeping the balls of his feet on the floor. It was early evening. I had not turned on the overhead lights in the office. The lamp on my desk was lit, and the rest of the illumination was the odd diffuse, ambient light of the Back Bay filtering through the snow. I poured some more coffee. We added whisky.

"What did you talk about?" Quirk said.

"Asked Husak who hired him to represent the Ukes," Hawk said.

"He tell you?"

"Un-huh."

"Willingly?" Quirk said.

Hawk smiled.

"He pretty willing," Hawk said.

"Why?" Quirk said.

"We just talkin'," Hawk said. "Right?"

"We're just three good old boys," Quirk said. "Sitting in a dim room, drinking whisky and looking at the weather."

"I stuck him out the window of his office a little," Hawk said.

"That would make him willing," Quirk said. "Who'd he say hired him?"

"Boots Podolak," Hawk said.

Quirk stopped rocking his chair. He held the coffee mug in both hands and inhaled the steam coming off the top before he drank some. Then he tilted his head back a little and let the coffee and whisky ease down his throat.

"Boots," Quirk said.

"You know him," I said.

"Yes. Husak say why Boots hired him?"

"See to it that nobody rolled on anybody," I said.

"You think he knew more than he told you?"

"He knew, he'da told," Hawk said.

Quirk nodded.

"High window," he said. "Did you talk to Duda?"

"Not yet," Hawk said.

Quirk was quiet for a bit. We waited. Whatever it was he knew, he'd get to it.

"Husak's dead," Quirk said. "And we can't find Duda."

"How'd he die," Hawk said.

"He was decapitated," Quirk said. "In his office. Lotta blood."

Decapitated?

"Somebody making a point," Hawk said.

Quirk nodded.

"Who they making it to?" I said.

"Maybe you," Quirk said.

"What about Duda?" I said. "Any leads?"

"I'm not expecting to find him alive," Quirk said. "Unless he bailed out early . . . and far."

"Husak told us he was in Miami," I said.

"Maybe he got lucky," Quirk said. "He say where in Miami, or why?"

"Said he took a week off and went to Miami. Was due back this week."

"I'll call Miami," Quirk said, "ask them to check the resort hotels."

"I'd check some of the dumps along Miami Beach first," Hawk said.

"You don't think they're high-steppers?" Quirk said.

"You seen the office," Hawk said.

Quirk stood now and went to stand beside Hawk and look down at the street.

"He is fucking up traffic," Quirk said, "isn't he."

"Un-huh."

Quirk glanced at Hawk and turned slowly and looked at me. His back was to the window now.

"Being a veteran police investigator, and a deep student of human character, I'm going to hazard a guess. You went to see Boots."

"Incredible," Hawk said.

"Yeah, it is," Quirk said. "You hang him out a window?"

"Nope," Hawk said. "I put a gun to his head."

"Jesus Christ," Quirk said. "Boots Podolak?"

"That sort of how he felt," Hawk said.

"What'd he tell you?"

"Well, it got kind of confusing. An alarm went off and there were cops and all I got was to ask Tony Marcus about his daughter."

"Tony Marcus?" Quirk said.

"There's some connection," I said. "Between them."

"Tony and Boots?" Quirk said. "Christ! Just when you think you've seen everything."

21

WE HAD LUNCH with Tony Marcus in his restaurant. The three of us sat in the front booth, near the door. The deep snow outside made the interior of the room seem brighter than usual.

"Sit you here for show," Tony said to me. "Try to attract a few white folks."

"Ebony and Ivory," I said.

"Damn straight," Tony said. "What you want for lunch? Fried chicken's good."

"Can I get watermelon with that?" I said.

Hawk grinned. Tony gestured to the waitress.

"Tell Roy," he said. "Put together a nice-tasting plate for these gentlemen. And bring me a Jack Daniel's."

He looked at us. Hawk and I both shook our heads.

"Guess I'm drinking alone," Tony said.

The waitress went away. Ty Bop stood near the front door, simultaneously motionless and edgy. Junior loomed at the end of the bar.

"You might get a more, ah, diversified patronage," I said, "if Ty Bop weren't standing there like a scorpion on the nod."

"Ty Bop like a son to me," Tony said. "How you getting on with the Ukrainians?"

"Went up to see Boots Podolak," Hawk said.

Tony frowned and shook his head.

"Don't know the name," he said.

The waitress set his drink down near his elbow and went silently away. She had cornrows and a very successful backside.

"Tha's odd," Hawk said. "He knew yours."

"Lotta people know mine," Tony said.

He took an appreciative drink of his whisky.

"Boots say we should ask you 'bout your daughter," Hawk said.

Tony finished sipping his whisky and set the glass down carefully where it had been. Nothing appeared to change. But the air felt suddenly brittle.

"Daughter?" Tony said.

"I ask Boots was there something going on with you and him, and he say ask him 'bout his daughter."

"Why would he say that?"

"I was, ah, urgin' him strongly," Hawk said.

"Why you even talking to him?" Tony said.

"He hired the lawyers represented the Ukrainians," Hawk said.

"I got nothin' to do with them," Tony said.

"'Cept for them trying to take away your business."

"They just nibblin' at the edges," Tony said.

The waitress with the cornrows came toward us from the kitchen with a large tray balanced at her shoulder. Tony looked up and saw her and waved her away. Without breaking stride she turned and walked back to the kitchen. I felt bad. I'd spotted ribs on the platter.

Hawk said, "I don't believe that, Tony."

Tony raised his glass and sipped some more whisky. He looked at Hawk silently for a time.

"With all due respect, Hawk," Tony said. "I don't actually give a fuck you believe me or you don't."

"You got a daughter?" Hawk said.

Tony looked at him silently.

"I ain't got nothing else to say, Hawk."

"This is silly," Hawk said. "I gonna find out, why not find it out from you."

"Known you a long time," Tony said to Hawk. "Paid you some money sometimes. Never had no problem with you."

"Now you do," Hawk said.

"You just missed dying once already in this thing," Tony said.

"What thing?" Hawk said.

Tony shook his head. By the door, Ty Bop was holding a long-barreled semiautomatic at his side. At the bar, Junior had produced a sawed-off shotgun. Two men came from the area where Tony had his office. Both had shotguns. The half a dozen or so diners in Ebony & Ivory sat frozen in their places, shoulders hunched, trying to be as small as they could be. Ready to hit the floor if the balloon went up. Hawk looked slowly around the room. Then he nodded to himself at the conclusion he reached, and stood and began to walk to the door. I followed him. In order for Hawk to open the door, Ty Bop would have to move a little. Hawk paid no attention. When he reached the door he opened it and Ty Bop took a half step out of the way. Hawk went through. I stopped for a moment and turned to Tony.

"This just isn't helping your diversity project," I said, and went out after Hawk.

Ty Bop closed the door behind me.

22

"WE'RE REALLY on a roll," I said to Hawk. "Everybody
we talk to is either dead or wants to kill us."

"'Cept maybe Zippity Duda."

"What's your guess?" I said.

"Him too," Hawk said.

Hawk drove as he did everything else, as if he were born
to do it. And the Navigator moved through the snow-clogged
traffic like a Porsche.

"Like to talk with them Ukrainians," Hawk said.

"They don't seem too welcoming," I said.

"Need a translator," Hawk said. "Like in Port City."

"I think Mei Ling, she was hot for you."

"'Course she was," Hawk said.

"Also, she was Chinese," I said.

"I noticed that," Hawk said.

"So she probably wouldn't do well with Ukrainian."

"You honkies always thinking up reasons why us black folks can't do what we wants."

"Wants?" I said.

"Ah is working on my accent," Hawk said.

"No need," I said. "I know you're black."

"Maybe Susan know somebody at Harvard," Hawk said.

"Cops got a guy from Harvard," I said.

"How long he last," Hawk said.

"Twenty minutes," I said.

Hawk nodded silently. We were westbound on Mass. Ave now, approaching the Back Bay.

"Well, be nice to have a translator 'case we come across something to translate."

We crossed Columbus Ave, past the community center where the Hi Hat once stood. I remembered it as being upstairs. Symphony Sid had done his radio show from there. Illinois Jacquette had played there. Across Columbus, we went past the Savoy, where I'd listened to Wild Bill Davidson, and across Huntington Ave, and on past Symphony Hall.

"Ives," I said.

"Ives?" Hawk said.

"The spook," I said.

"What about him?"

We stopped for the light at Boylston Street. It was as law-abiding as Hawk ever got.

"He'll know somebody speaks Ukrainian," I said.

"And he going to help us out, why?" Hawk said.

"Because he thinks we're a couple of righteous guys?"

"Sure he do," Hawk said.

The light changed. We crossed Boylston.

"I'll talk to him," I said.

At Beacon Street, Hawk turned left and after another block or so went up the ramp to Storrow Drive where we headed west past B.U. along the river.

"I gather we're not picking up Cecile," I said.

"She say she'll meet us at Susan's," Hawk said.

On our right, the river was mostly frozen over, with maybe a little open water here and there in the middle. The snow on the frozen parts was already beginning to grime, and the open water in the middle looked iron-cold.

"Be nice to find out a little about Tony's daughter," I said.

"Would," Hawk said.

"If he's got a daughter."

"If," Hawk said.

"Know anything about that?"

"No," Hawk said. "You?"

"How the hell would I know?" I said. "I'm the white guy."

"Oh, yes," Hawk said. "Thank you so much for reminding me."

The ugly elevation of the Mass Pike was to our left, and beyond it what used to be Braves Field, now part of B.U., with high rise dorms built around it. There used to be a ballpark right there.

"He got an ex-wife," Hawk said.

"She have a daughter?"

"Don't know," Hawk said. "She's a lesbian."

"Really?" I said. "She know that when she married Tony?"

"Don't think either of them did," Hawk said.

"You know where the ex-wife is?"

"I know people who know."

"Maybe you should ask them."

"By heavens," Hawk said. "I think I shall."

"Christ," I said. "One minute Stepinfetchit. The next Noël Coward."

"Ah embraces diversity," Hawk said.

We went over the Anderson Bridge and skirted Harvard Square. In another five minutes we pulled into Susan's driveway, which someone had thoughtfully plowed.

"She ain't going to cook, is she?" Hawk said.

"I hope not," I said. "Can Cecile cook?"

"I don't know," Hawk said.

"Let's hope for order out," I said.

23

IVES WAS IN South Boston now, just across Ft. Point Channel, in the new Federal Courthouse on Fan Pier. Everyone had to go through metal detectors to go upstairs in the courthouse, so I locked my gun in the glove compartment of my car and risked it unarmed.

I passed security with high honors and took the elevator to Ives's floor. Black letters on the otherwise blank pebbled glass door said COUNSELRY INTEGRATION ADVISERS. Ives had a special sense of humor. When I opened the door, a good-looking silver-haired woman of some seniority was at the reception desk, wearing a deeply serious suit. Her desk was bare. The room was bare. No windows. No paintings. No signs. There was an overhead light.

"Spenser," I said. "For Ives."

She smiled noncommittally and picked up the phone and dialed.

"Spenser, sir."

She listened for a moment and hung up the phone.

"He'll be down to get you in a moment, Mr. Spenser."

"Thank you."

I would have sat, but there were no chairs. A door behind the woman opened and Ives was there.

"Well," he said. "Young Lochinvar."

He invited me to join him by nodding his head, and I followed him through the door and down a corridor past narrow, unmarked doors, to a corner office with a grandiose view of Boston Harbor and the city. He gestured me toward a large black leather chair with a lot of brass nail heads.

"Drink?" he said.

I shook my head.

"Well, my trusty companion," he said. "You look well. Fully recovered, are we?"

Ives had the unfeigned sincerity of a coffin salesman. He was thin and tallish and three-buttoned and natural-shouldered. His sandy hair, tinged now with gray, was long and combed back. He looked like a poet. If you had never met one. The last time we had done business, I had almost died.

"I'm fine."

"So," Ives said, looking out the window at his view, "what brings you to my place of business."

So much for the small talk.

"I need a tough guy who is fluent in Ukrainian."

Ives smiled.

"Who doesn't," he said.

"I thought, given your line of work, you might have encountered someone."

"In my line of work," Ives said, "I have encountered almost everyone."

I nodded and waited.

"Ukrainians are a savage people," Ives said. "Did you know that during the Second World War there was a Ukrainian SS unit."

"I knew that," I said.

"The Ukrainians one might meet in your line of endeavor hold promise of being the very worst kind."

"The very worst," I said.

"How is your African-American colleague?" Ives said.

"No need to show off," I said. "I already know you don't miss much."

Ives smiled.

"It is my profession," he said.

"Translator?" I said.

"I know someone," Ives said, "but it is a bit of a, ah, situation."

"I'll be brave," I said.

"You recall several years ago you were almost killed by a man calling himself, at the time, Rugar."

"The Gray Man," I said.

"Once you recovered, you retaliated, I believe by apprehending him and threatening him with prison."

"We made a deal," I said.

"He speaks Ukrainian."

"Rugar's Ukrainian?"

"I don't know his nationality. Nor is Rugar his current name. But he speaks many languages, and he is not afraid of Ukrainians."

"Nor much else," I said.

"I might be able to arrange a meeting."

"Do," I said.

"Your past relationship will not interfere?"

"Not on my account."

"And perhaps not on his," Ives said. "The Gray Man is, after all, a professional."

"Aren't we all," I said.

24

———•———

THE GRAY MAN wanted a public place, so Hawk and I met him in the central rotunda at Quincy Market. It was a high-domed circular space in the center of the old market building. There were tables and benches for eating. Food stalls occupied both the wings that ran off the rotunda, and the room was normally full of tourists and high-school kids from Melrose. Hawk and I were drinking coffee at a table next to a wall where we could see the whole space.

And there he came.

He was still gray, a gray trench coat, gray slacks, black

shoes, his gray hair smoothed back, his gray turtleneck showing at the top of his trench coat. He was still tall, and he still wore an emerald in his right earlobe. He walked straight across the floor of the rotunda and sat down at the table across from Hawk and me.

"No one has killed you yet," he said to me.

Hawk looked at him without expression.

"You've come the closest," I said. "We still calling you Rugar?"

He shrugged. "Might as well."

"You speak Ukrainian?" I said.

"Yes," Rugar said.

If he was aware of Hawk's stare, he didn't show it. He showed nothing. He seemed to feel nothing. He moved only as required and then with great economy of motion.

"You know me?" Hawk said to Rugar.

"Hawk."

"You scared of trouble?" Hawk said.

"No," Rugar said.

"What's your ask," Hawk said.

"To translate only?" Rugar said.

"Yes."

"No other duties?"

"Other duties be up to you," Hawk said. "I'm hiring you to translate."

Rugar gave him a price.

"Okay," Hawk said.

Rugar looked at me.

"You're in this?"

"Yes."

"You have no problem with me?"

"No."

"And I have none with you."

"We could join hands," I said, "and dance around the table."

"You got a right to know," Hawk said. "Be a lotta shooting, sooner or later."

Rugar nodded.

"Ain't hiring you to jump in," Hawk said.

"I understand."

"You want to jump in, be sure it on our side."

Rugar's face moved slightly. He might have been smiling.

"Fair enough," he said.

25

A WARM RAIN was depreciating the plowed snow, which had long since turned ugly anyway. Hawk parked on a hydrant on Cambridge Street. He and I strolled through the construction near MGH and turned up Charles Street with our coat collars turned rakishly up. Both of us wore raincoats. Mine was glistening black with a zipper front. Hawk was going with the more conventional Burberry trench. I had on a Pittsburg Pirates baseball cap. Hawk had a San Francisco Giants cap, which he wore backwards.

"Aren't you a little long in the tooth to be wearing your hat backwards?" I said.

"I was younger," Hawk said, "I be wearing it sideways."

We turned left and went uphill a block on Revere Street. Like most of Beacon Hill, it was lined with red brick buildings, which were mostly four-story town houses. The one we stopped at had a front door painted a shiny black, with a peephole and a big, polished brass door handle. Hawk rang the bell and stood where he could be seen through the peephole. In a moment the door opened narrowly, on a chain bolt. A black woman wearing big eyeglasses with green frames looked out.

"Yes?"

"Natalie Marcus?" Hawk said.

"Goddard," she said.

Hawk nodded and smiled.

"Natalie Goddard," he said.

When he really juiced it, the smile was amazing. It created the illusion of warmth and friendship and genuine personal regard.

"My name is Hawk," he said. "I need to talk with you about Tony's daughter."

"What makes you think I know anything about her?" the woman said.

"I know you were once married to Tony. Seemed reasonable."

"She is not my daughter," Natalie said.

Natalie had a careful WASP drawl, which seemed odd in someone as clearly not a WASP as she was.

"Could we come in out of the rain?" Hawk said. "Talk about it in the foyer, perhaps?"

Hawk is a wonderful mimic, and I thought he might be picking up her accent. She looked at me.

"And this gentleman?"

"My assistant," Hawk said. "His name is Spenser."

Hawk smiled at her again. She did nothing for a moment.

Then she said, "There's no need to come in. I can talk with you right here."

"As you wish," Hawk said.

I knew he was disappointed. He didn't mind the rain, but he hated to have the full smile rejected.

"So how old is Dolores now?" Hawk said.

"Dolores?"

"Do I have it wrong?" Hawk said.

"I thought you knew her."

Hawk looked embarrassed.

"I do, but . . . names . . . I'm terribly embarrassed."

"Jolene," Natalie said.

"Of course," Hawk said with a big smile. "Dolores . . . Jolene . . . an easy mistake."

Natalie smiled slightly.

"How old would Jolene be now?" Hawk said.

"I was with Tony ten years ago. . . ." She did some silent math. "She'd be twenty-four now."

"She live with Tony?"

"Not with her mother."

"They divorced?"

"Tony and Veronica? I don't think they were ever married."

"But Tony acknowledges Jolene as his."

"Oh, yeah," Natalie said.

The *yeah* slipped out as if Natalie had shifted into another language.

"Why 'Oh, yeah'?" Hawk said.

"Tony never loved anything in his life. And he decides to love Jolene."

"What's wrong with Jolene?" Hawk said.

The rain was steady. Everything glistened, including my stunning black zip-front raincoat. Cars moved narrowly past us on Revere Street.

"Everything is wrong with Jolene," Natalie said. "Drugs, sex, alcohol, rebellion, disdain. He has spoiled her beyond fucking recognition."

Maybe the foreign language was her native tongue.

"Where does she live?" Hawk said.

"With her current husband, I suppose."

"Heavens," Hawk said. "I didn't even know she was married."

"Maybe she isn't, but I think she is; either way, she's living with Brock."

"Brock?" Hawk said.

"Brock Rimbaud," she said. "I've heard he's worse than she is."

"Do you know where they live?"

"On the waterfront somewhere."

"You wouldn't have an address?"

"Oh, God, no," she said. "I've had no connection, to Tony or his hideous family, in years."

I was not buying that.

Natalie appeared to see that as an interview-ending remark, because she closed the door after she said it.

"Brock Rimbaud?" I said.

"Don't sound like no brother," Hawk said

"Maybe he changed his name," I said. "Trying to pass."

"What you think his real name is?" Hawk said.

"Old Black Joe?" I said.

"Mostly they ain't naming us that no more," Hawk said.

We walked back down Revere Street in the melting rain. I hunched my shoulders a little as a drop of water wormed down inside my collar on the back of my neck. Maybe wearing his hat bill backward was more than a fashion statement on Hawk's part. I grinned at him as we reached Charles Street.

"Smile didn't work," I said. "Did it."

"Just prove she a lesbian," Hawk said.

26

———•———

SPENSER'S CRIME-STOPPER tip number 31: If you have a name and no address, try looking in the phone book. I did, and there they were. Brock and Jolene Rimbaud, it said proudly, with a Rowes Wharf address. Hawk and I went down there. For the second straight day, it was raining. The Big Dig was still everywhere, as they began to dismantle the aging ironwork of the old elevated expressway.

The Rowes Wharf condos were part of a big handsome complex on the waterfront that included a huge archway and the Boston Harbor Hotel. In the lobby of Rimbaud's building was a security guy in a blue blazer and striped tie. Hawk asked him for the Rimbauds.

"May I say who is calling?"

"Say we from Mr. Marcus," Hawk said.

The guard dialed the phone and spoke into it and hung up.

"Through that door," he said, "down the steps, turn right, second condo."

We went. The door led outside. We were on a boat slip. To our right, a promenade led past the big archway, to the hotel. In good weather, people sat outside on the promenade and drank flavored martinis and ate light meals and listened to live music. In the cold rain, the promenade was empty except for one guy in a fashionable yellow slicker, trying to hold an umbrella over a miserable little white dog whose hairdo was being seriously compromised as they walked toward the archway. We walked up the two steps at the Rimbaud condo and rang the bell. The door opened and it was Brock himself. He looked like the cover of a romance novel. Shoulder-length blond hair, pale blue eyes, chiseled features, pouty lips, his flowered shirt unbuttoned halfway down his manly upper body. He stood so that his right hand was concealed behind the door.

Hawk said, "My name's Hawk. This is Spenser. We need to talk."

"Tony send you?" Brock said.

"'Course he did," Hawk said. "It's raining."

"I don't give a fuck what it's doing," Brock said. "You come in when I know why you want to."

A good-looking young woman with coffee-colored skin appeared behind Rimbaud. Her hair was in an elaborate pattern of tight cornrows. Ethnic as hell.

"Who is it, Brock?" she said, and pressed her considerable boobs against his left arm.

"Couple dudes say they from your old man," Rimbaud said.

Jolene was barefoot and a little big for her clothes. She looked to be a size six. Her jeans appeared to be a size two. They ended well below her navel. Her cropped tank top ended well above. She had a nice, flat stomach, and her arms and shoulders looked strong.

"I don't know them," she said.

"Well, my heavens," Hawk said. "Look at how you've grown, girl. I knew Veronica and Tony when you was born, child. And look what you turned out to be."

I looked at Hawk. He was thrilled to see her. He was folksy. I felt a little nauseous.

"You know my mom, too?" Jolene said.

"Huh-unh."

"Oh, Brock, let them in," Jolene said. "They seem nice."

Brock nodded us in. Anything the little lady wants. As we came in he put the gun he'd been concealing behind the door into his belt. He saw me see him do it, and he met my look.

"My line of work," he said. "Pays to be careful."

Jolene went across the living room to the couch. It was

less than a flounce but certainly more than a walk. On the low table in front of the couch there was a bottle of Riesling in an ice bucket, and two glasses, half empty. Or half full. There was some kind of fusion jazz playing on the stereo. I hated fusion jazz. Brock went and stood near Jolene. I stood near the door. Hawk sat on a big, red, tasseled hassock in front of them. Nobody offered us a drink. Nobody turned down the fusion. Through the big picture window, I could see the rain dappling the gray water of the harbor.

"Tell us about you and Boots Podolak," Hawk said to Jolene.

"What kind of a fucking question is that," Brock said.

"Who's Boots Podolak?" Jolene said.

"Shut up, Jolene," Brock said.

"Who you telling to shut up?" Jolene said.

"There some other fucking Jolene in here," Brock said. "I don't want you talking to these bozos."

"Bozos?" I said to Hawk.

Hawk shrugged. Brock took the gun out of his waistband.

"Don't you go pointing no gun in my house, you mother-fucker," Jolene said.

"Get out," Brock said, "Right now, or I'll blow your mother-fucking heads off."

"What's goin' on," Jolene said.

"Keep fucking quiet," Brock said.

"You the one gonna get your mother-fucking head blown off," Jolene said, "my daddy hear you talk to me like that."

The gun was a nine-millimeter. He had thumbed the hammer back.

"Shut up, bitch," he said, and raised the gun.

Hawk stood.

"Don't mean to start up no domestic dispute," he said.

I opened the door. Hawk smiled at them.

Hawk said, "We'll be seeing you all again real soon, I hope."

"Fuck you," Jolene said.

We went out and closed the door. They were screaming at each other behind us.

"Look at how you've grown, girl," I said.

"Got us in there, didn't it?" Hawk said.

"Not for long," I said. "And as we left, I believe I heard a fuck you."

"I believe she talking to you," Hawk said.

"No doubt," I said. "Well, we learned there's something up with Boots."

"And Jolene don't know what."

"And Brock thinks he's tough."

"And we was right," Hawk said. "I don't think Brock a brother."

"By God, you're right," I said. "Mission accomplished."

27

IT WAS DARK and wet and grim in the Public Gardens when Hawk and I met Tony Marcus on the small footbridge that spanned the Swan Boat Lake. The lake was drained, and the swan boats huddled miserably against their boarding dock under the mixed drizzle of rain and sleet. Tony had on a big, soft hat with a wide brim. The fur collar on his tweed overcoat was turned up. His hands were pushed down into his coat pockets, and a big, long, black silk scarf wrapped around his neck and hung down along the button closure of the coat. At the Arlington Street end of the bridge, Ty

Bop hunched miserably next to Junior, as if he was taking shelter from the weather. Junior was wearing a big fur hat with earflaps. It appeared to be the only concession he had made to the weather. Other than the hat, as far as I could see, he didn't know there was weather. At the Charles Street end of the footbridge was a guy named Leonard, who was Tony's number-two guy. It was hard to see him in the late-afternoon gloom, but I knew that Leonard was very black, with good cheekbones. He shaved his head like Hawk. He wore a moustache and goatee, and he always smelled of very good cologne. He wasn't as good a shooter as Ty Bop, and he didn't have as much muscle as Junior. But he was a very successful combination of both.

"The weather sucks," Tony said. "This better be worth it."

"I give you two words," Hawk said. "Jolene Marcus."

Tony showed no reaction.

"What about her?" he said.

"She married outside the faith," Hawk said.

"What about her," Tony said again.

"Whassup," Hawk said, "with her husband and Boots Podolak?"

I was wearing my black nylon raincoat with the cool zipper front. I had my hands in my pockets. In the right pocket was my Browning nine-millimeter. I kept my hand on the butt, my thumb on the hammer. I could cock it before it cleared my pocket. I'd practiced. There were people hurrying through the gardens on their way home from work, and some of them came across the bridge. But there were no casual walkers in the mean weather.

Tony looked at Hawk as if he were appraising him for auction. Hawk waited. I watched Ty Bop. Ty Bop was the shooter. Junior probably would have an Uzi, maybe a Bull Pup, under his coat. But it wasn't second nature to him the way it was with Ty Bop. Leonard would have a handgun, and he'd be good with it. But for Ty Bop, shooting was a part of his viscera. It was who he was. Ty Bop was the one to kill first.

"Whadya know?" Tony finally said in a soft voice.

"I know she your daughter with Veronica," Hawk said. "I know she married to a horse's ass."

"You seen them?" Tony said.

His voice was even softer.

"Yes."

"Where?"

"Rowes Wharf," Hawk said.

"You went to her house?"

I hunched my shoulders slightly.

"I did," Hawk said.

I could hear Tony breathe deeply through his nose.

"What did she say?"

I could feel the tightness begin to loosen in my trapezius.

"She don't seem to know nothing 'bout Boots," Hawk said.

"Brock?"

"He did," Hawk said. "Pulled a gun. Told us to, ah believe, get the fuck out."

"He pulled a gun on you," Tony said.

"Un-huh."

"You let it slide?"

"Un-huh. They started shoutin' at each other and me and my trusted companion here dee-parted."

Tony was silent. He glanced down the bridge toward Ty Bop and Junior. He looked the other way at Leonard. He raised his voice slightly.

"Go wait in the car," he said.

Junior and Leonard looked pleased. Ty Bop seemed disappointed. When they were gone, Tony took his hands out of his pockets and leaned his forearms on the bridge railing and looked down at the empty lake bottom.

"Her mother's no good, never was. I wasn't married to her. Just fucked her some. Knocked her up. When the kid was born, I took her. Jolene's twenty. I sent her to fucking Hampshire College. She's had two abortions."

He paused. I wondered if there was a connection between Hampshire and abortions. Hawk didn't say anything. The sleety rain drizzled down, not very hard and not very fast, but steady.

"Thirty thousand a year," Tony said, "and she's the old joke. Only fucked for friends, didn't have an enemy in the world."

It was hard language. If you told it tough, maybe it was

less painful. Tony kept staring down, nodding his head softly, as if to himself.

"Then this honkie jerk-off comes along and she decide he the one. First time I see him I know what he is. But he what she wants. So she marries him. I set him up with a nice little book in the South End, easy living, no deadbeats. But he can't hack it. Refuses to pay off on a bet, smacks the customer around when the customer complains. Customer complains to the cops. We got to shut down the book for a while. I set him up someplace else . . . same long story. Asshole can't make a living. But she loves him. Somebody else, I have Ty Bop kill him, but . . ."

"So what about Boots," Hawk said.

It was dark now. The lights on Boylston Street were amorphous in the drizzle.

"Dumbass kid decides he's going to acquire new territory for us."

"You and him?" Hawk said.

"Yeah. Show me the kind of fucking criminal genius he is. So he decides to set us up in Marshport. Says it's a black population run by a few fucking Bohunks. Says they'll welcome us in, we get a foothold."

"And what did he think the Bohunks be doing," Hawk said, "while he getting this foothold?"

"He don't think, Hawk. He a fucking airhead. He think pumping iron and carrying a gun make him a tough guy."

"You weren't able to explain that it didn't," Hawk said.

"Jolene say I don't want him to succeed, that I, ah, repressing him. I told you she been to college."

"You let him use some soldiers," Hawk said.

"Sure, but I don't want no big war with Boots Podolak," Tony said. "For Marshport? What kind of business plan is that?"

Tony shook his head.

"So?" Hawk said.

"So I make a deal with Boots," Tony said. "He lets the kid grab a little piece of Marshport so Jolene can think he got a dick."

"And you let Boots grab a little piece of your enterprise," Hawk said.

Looking down at the empty pond bed, Tony nodded yes.

"And," Hawk said, "maybe you and Boots can designate who gets the short straw in your neighborhoods."

Tony nodded again.

"And Luther Gillespie gets aced."

Tony nodded again. We were all quiet.

After a time, Hawk said, "Known you a long time, Tony."

"Yeah."

"Don't want to give you more trouble than you got."

Tony nodded.

"But I got to even up for Luther Gillespie and his family, you understand that."

"And I got to look out for my daughter," Tony said.

"I got no interest in hurting her," Hawk said.

"She wants something, I do what I gotta do to get it for her," Tony said. "Right now she wants her husband to be a player in Marshport."

"I can work around you on this," Hawk said, "I will."

"I'll do the same," Tony said.

"If I can't . . ." Hawk said.

"You can't," Tony said.

"So we know," Hawk said.

"We know," Tony said.

28

HAWK AND I walked in the rain up Boylston Street to my office. I broke out the Irish whisky and poured us two generous shots.

"So how do you want to do this?" I said.

"Gonna go right at the Ukes," Hawk said. "Leave Rimbaud to do whatever he gonna do."

"Ukes probably don't make fine distinctions," I said. "They have trouble on their end, they'll make trouble at Brock's end."

"Which means maybe we have trouble with Tony," Hawk said.

"I don't think Clauswicz was in favor of fighting a two-front war," I said.

"Got no choice," Hawk said.

The whisky was warm and pleasant in my throat. The rain came steady against the office window.

"You think Brock's going to settle for the little piece of Marshport that Boots will give him?"

"Too stupid," Hawk said.

"You bet," I said.

"So he'll keep taking more from Boots," Hawk said. "And Boots be taking more from Tony."

"Which isn't going to work in the long run."

"No."

"So sooner or later there will be a war," I said. "With us or without us."

"Less we take out the Ukes," Hawk said.

"Then the kid gets Marshport," I said.

"Not for long," Hawk said.

"No," I said. "He's too stupid."

"And he don't know it," Hawk said. "And he ain't tough. And he don't know that, either."

"Deadly combination," I said.

"Tony's only hope would be to take it away from him," Hawk said.

"Or hope the daughter gets over him."

"Be easy to do," Hawk said.

"Maybe not for her," I said.

"Gonna have a lot of people mad at us," Hawk said.

"We'll get over it," I said.

"Ain't really your fight," Hawk said.

We each drank another swallow of whisky. The rain came steady on the black window.

"Yeah," I said. "It is."

Hawk was quiet for a time, then he nodded his head slowly.

"Yeah," he said. "It is."

I got up and looked out my window. Berkeley Street was dark and shiny wet and empty. A few cars went by on Boylston Street. And once in a while there was somebody walking, bent forward, hunched against the rain, hands in pockets. Genderless in the dark weather.

"Can't let it go," Hawk said.

"I know."

"Gonna be a bad mess any way it plays," Hawk said.

"Certainly will," I said.

"So, I guess we may as well do what we gonna do and not think too much 'bout what everybody else gonna do," Hawk said.

"Isn't that what we always do?" I said.

"It is," Hawk said.

29

WE TOOK my car this time, which no one would recognize, and sat in it, up the street from the Ukrainian fortress on Market Street in Marshport. The rain had gone, and the cold that had come in behind it was formidable. My motor was idling and the heater was on high. The outside temperature registered six on my dashboard thermometer.

"Why is it again we live 'round here?" Hawk said.

"We like the seasonal change," I said.

The street was nearly empty. A stumblebum in many layers of cast-off clothing inched his way up Market Street. He stopped to stare down into a trash barrel and then moved on. Several windows in the three-deckers on both sides of the street were boarded over. There were no dogs, no children. Just the solitary bum shuffling numbly along.

"Think it's colder in the poor neighborhoods?" I said.

"Yes," Hawk said.

"Because God favors the rich?"

"Why they rich," Hawk said.

"It is easier," I said, "for a camel to pass through the eye of a needle, than . . ."

"Here they come," Hawk said.

Two men wearing overcoats and watch caps came out of the stronghold and got into a Chevrolet Suburban. We saw the plume of exhaust from the tailpipe as the car started up. We all sat for a time while the defroster cleared the windows on the Chevy. Then it rolled forward and went toward Marshport Road. We let them get far ahead and cruised out after them. There were some cars on the road, and when we turned onto Route 1A there were more. On open highway, it's easy to stay with the car you're tailing but harder to avoid being seen. In the city it's easy to stay unseen, but more difficult not to lose the tailee. Fortunately I was nationally ranked in both modes, and when the Ukrainians pulled up in front of a used-furniture store on Blue Hill Ave, they thought they were alone.

The store was in the first floor of a three-story wooden building with peeling gray paint. There was a liquor store on one side, and an appliance repair shop on the other. The store looked as if it had once sold groceries. The big windows in the front were frosted with the cold. A big sign pasted inside the half window of the front door read USED AND NEW FURNITURE: BUY OR RENT. An old maroon Dodge van was parked on the street in front of the store. It had no hubcaps. The Ukes double-parked their Suburban beside it and walked to the store, leaving the motor running. As they walked toward the store, one of the two men absently beeped the remote door lock device on his key chain. The taillights flashed once. The men went into the furniture store.

"We need to be pretty close behind them," Hawk said. "They don't look like they planning to stay long."

Hawk got out of the car. He had his big .44 Mag in his right hand. I got out my .38. There appeared to be only two guys, and I was sentimental about the little revolver. Hawk walked through the front door as if he was walking onto a yacht. The big .44 hung straight down by his right side. I glanced in both directions before I went in after him. Inside, behind the counter, a short, plump black man holding a sawed-off baseball bat was trying to keep his body between his wife and the two big white men. As we came in, one of the white men gestured at the baseball bat and laughed, and patted his leather coat over the belt area. He said something to his partner in a language not my own.

A small bell jingled on the door as it closed behind us, and both white men turned. I moved away from Hawk. Two targets are harder than one. The four of us stood looking at each other.

"S'happenin'?" Hawk said.

No one spoke. Hawk looked at the short black man.

"My name's Hawk," he said. "I'm on your side."

"Man says we sign this store over to him or he gonna kill us both. Her first."

The two white men looked at us with contempt. The one with the leather coat said to us, "Go way," and gestured toward the door. Hawk looked closely at both the big white men.

"Danylko Levkovych?" he said.

The man in the leather coat said, "Ya."

Without a word, Hawk raised the .44 Mag and shot him in the forehead. The man fell backward and lay dead on the floor with his head propped against the dirty green wall of the little store. The only sound was the silent resonance of the recent explosion and the woman, still shielded by her husband, whimpering softly. Hawk had already shifted the gun onto the second white man before the one in leather had hit the floor. The second man stared at Hawk with no expression. Most people are afraid of dying. If this guy was, he gave no sign.

"You speak English?" Hawk said to him.

The man didn't speak or move. He just kept looking at Hawk.

"He talked English to me," the shop owner said.

He was still holding the sawed-off bat, for which he had no use—and, in fact, never had. Hawk looked at the second white man. The white man looked back.

"Fadeyushka Badyrka?" Hawk said.

The man nodded.

"You know who I am," Hawk said.

The man shrugged.

"I was the guy protecting Luther Gillespie," Hawk said.

The man smiled faintly.

"I gonna kill you next," Hawk said.

The man continued to smile faintly.

"But not now," Hawk said.

He jerked his thumb toward the door.

"Beat it," he said.

The man shrugged slightly and walked straight past us and out the front door without ever looking at his partner on the floor. He beeped the car doors open and got in and drove away.

"I don't think we scared him," I said.

"No."

Hawk looked at the store owner.

"You been having any argument lately with Tony Marcus?" he said.

"I don't work with Tony anymore," the store owner said.

Hawk nodded.

"I gonna clean this up," he said. "But it gonna take a while. I was you I'd take the missus to a warm climate for a while."

"And what happens to my business?"

"Same thing will happen if you dead," Hawk said.

"You think they be back?"

"They be back," Hawk said. "I ain't always gonna be here."

The store owner nodded. His wife had stopped crying.

"We'll go to my sister," she said.

Her husband looked like dying might be better.

"Go there," Hawk said.

"It's in Arkansas," the store owner said.

Hawk grinned.

"Go there anyway," he said.

And we left.

In the car, I said, "That's why you didn't shoot him."

"What's why?"

"Because he wasn't scared," I said.

"Killing somebody ain't afraid to die ain't much justice," Hawk said.

"Or revenge," I said.

"I trying to get things back in balance," Hawk said. "That seem like justice to me."

"When you do it, it's revenge," I said. "When the state does it, it's society's revenge."

"Which it call justice," Hawk said.

"Exactly," I said. "Change places and handy-dandy."

Hawk grinned at me.

"Which be the justice," he said. "Which be the thief?"

"I think Shakespeare used *is*," I said. "Which *is* the justice."

"Shakespeare wasn't no brother," Hawk said.

"I knew that," I said.

30

———•———

HAWK AND I went back to my office and had a couple of beers together in the empty building, looking down from my window on the near-empty intersection.

"That didn't do much for anybody," Hawk said.

"Saved the storekeeper's ass," I said.

Hawk grunted.

"Storekeeper," he said. "Man runs a book out of there. Ukies didn't want the store, they wanted the book."

"What I haven't figured out," I said, "since this started, does Boots or whoever's running the enterprise think he can take over the crime commerce in an all-black neighborhood and staff it with white guys from Central Europe and the people will keep right on coming?"

"Maybe got a few Uncle Drobits for staffing," Hawk said. "Truth is, it don't matter. Some black people be more comfortable with a brother, but not all of them. Some black people figure you be a brother you can't be very good."

"You're so smart, why aren't you white?" I said.

Hawk nodded.

"And people need a bookie or a pimp or a guy to sell them blow, they generally need it bad enough so they do business with whoever's at the window. They want to place a bet and the only bookie there is Joseph Stalin"—Hawk shrugged—"they place the bet with Joe."

"The greater leveler," I said.

"Need," Hawk said.

"Yep."

We were quiet, sipping the beer, looking at the city-lit night.

"Now what," I said.

"We let the surviving Uke go back and tell what happened and we see what develops."

"Got anything longer-range than that?" I said.

"I thinking about taking Boots down, put a stop to the whole thing."

"And liberate Marshport?" I said.

"Yeah, sure," Hawk said. "That too. You talk to Vinnie?"

"I've got him on standby."

"Might need him," Hawk said.

"I thought you didn't want him."

"Didn't want him protecting me," Hawk said. "Liberatin' Marshport be different."

"How Tony going to be feeling 'bout this?" I said.

Hawk stared at me.

"How come you talking funny?" he said.

"Been spending too much time with you."

"No such thing as too much time with me," Hawk said.

"So how's Tony going to react to this?" I said.

"Don't know," Hawk said.

"We don't want to fight a two-front war," I said.

" 'Less we have to."

"Think about it from where Tony's standing," I said. "He doesn't like Podolak any better than anyone else does. He's just allied so his son-in-law can feel like a big shot and his daughter won't be widowed."

"None of that my problem," Hawk said.

"So you knock off one of the Ukulele soldiers and Podolak will see it as not part of the deal."

"And Podolak get on Tony's case. Tony supposed to protect the Ukes, like Podolak s'posed to protect . . . what's that kid's name?"

"How could you forget," I said. "Brock Rimbaud."

"Yeah. But if I tell Tony I ain't killing no more street soldiers, Tony takes credit for it, and all be well."

"And when Podolak's ready to fall over," I said, "Tony might even help you push."

"So we don't fight Tony. We get him on our side."

"For the moment."

"Like Hitler and Stalin and the nonaggression pact," Hawk said.

"How you know about Hitler and Stalin," I said.

"Heard some white guys talking," Hawk said.

"Think Tony will buy it?" I said.

"Sure," Hawk said. "Easier than fighting us about it."

"You think?" I said.

"We hard to fight," Hawk said.

"But oh so easy to love," I said.

I went to the refrigerator and got out two more cans of beer. It was late. I stood beside Hawk and looked down at the quiet street. A yellow cab cruised down Boylston Street. Probably going to the Four Seasons.

"So if Tony buys it," I said, "all we got to do is go up to Marshport and take over the city."

"That be the plan," Hawk said.

"Any operational details?" I said. "Like, how?"

"I already give you the big picture," Hawk said. "You supposed to contribute something."

"How about I learn to say 'don't shoot' in Ukrainian?" I said.

31

───●───

WE ROLLED SLOWLY along Revere Beach Boulevard, looking for a parking spot. The spring was too early for there to be a lot of people at the beach, and Hawk pulled in half a block from the small pavilion on the beachfront where we were meeting Tony and Boots.

We sat in the car and looked at the meeting site.

"Tony buys it," Hawk said. "But he want to be sure Boots buy it, and Boots wants this meeting."

"Ty Bop and Junior," I said.

Hawk nodded.

"Leaning on the front fender of the black Escalade," he said. "Junior liable to break it."

A silver Mercedes sedan pulled up and double-parked by the pavilion. There were two Marshport police cars with it, fore and aft.

"That would be Boots," I said.

"With escort," Hawk said.

"He is the mayor of Marshport," I said.

Hawk grinned at me.

"So far," he said.

Four Marshport cops got out of the police cars and walked to the pavilion, and stood, one in each corner, and waited. Tony got out of the Escalade and walked to the pavilion with Leonard, the handsome black guy we'd met before. Leonard was wearing a dark cashmere overcoat that fitted him perfectly. You know you're with a clothes guy when he gets his overcoats made.

"Our turn," Hawk said. "Boots like to make the grand entrance."

It was breezy on the beachfront, and I wanted to zip up my leather jacket, but it would have meant zipping my gun inside the jacket, so I settled for shivering a little. Hawk showed no sign of cold. He never did. He never seemed hot, either. Mortality rested very lightly on him. As we passed Ty Bop, I pretended to shoot him, dropping my thumb on my forefinger. Junior smiled faintly. Ty Bop ignored me. He may not have even seen me as he stood, jittering in place by the big SUV, thinking long thoughts about shooting somebody.

"Kid gets any skinnier," I said to Hawk, "his gun will be shooting him."

"Don't be dissing Ty Bop," Hawk said. "Ain't many people can shoot better."

"Or more willingly," I said.

"Yeah," Hawk said. "Ty Bop like the work."

We stepped into the pavilion with Tony and Leonard and the four Marshport cops. As soon as we did, Boots stepped out of his Mercedes. With him was Fadeyushka Badyrka, the big Ukrainian gunboat that Hawk had declined to kill.

"We may be forming a lasting friendship with Fade-yushka," Hawk said.

"Remembering his name is a good start," I said.

It was early April and cool with the wind coming off the water. But Boots was dressed for deep January. He had on a fur-lined cap with earflaps that tied under the chin, and a heavy, dark, woolen overcoat with a black mouton collar snuggled up under his mean chin. His hands were in his pockets. His narrow shoulders were hunched. He walked straight up to Hawk and stood about a foot away.

"Okay," he said, "tell me."

I was standing a little back from Hawk and Boots and Tony, trying to find a spot where I could be useful if the ball went up. It was hard to find a place where someone couldn't shoot me dead. But it almost always is, if you think about it. I did what I could. I noticed that Leonard was having the same locational problems. The cops at each corner of the pavilion were sort of an issue for both of us. There were a few people on the beach. Some were walking dogs or small children, or both. Some were picking up things. I was never quite clear on what it was that people collected on beaches. No one paid any attention to the group in the pavilion.

"I shot one of your people," Hawk said. "Not realizin' he under Tony's protection. Apologize for that. Told Tony and I'll tell you. Long as you and Tony got a deal goin', I honor it."

"What kind of deal you think Tony and I got," Boots said.

"Don't know," Hawk said, "don't care. Tony says your people are protected. That be my deal."

Fadeyushka was looking at Hawk. I was looking at Fadeyushka. So was the handsome guy with Tony.

"You agree with that?" Boots said to Tony.

Tony nodded.

"Speak up," Boots said.

"I agree," Tony said.

I knew Tony wanted to kick Boots right out into the traffic on Revere Beach Boulevard, but he didn't show it. He seemed almost respectful when he spoke to Boots. Which I knew to be a crock. Nobody respected Boots. People were afraid of him, and with good reason. But it had little to do with respect. I was pretty sure Boots didn't know about this distinction, and if he did know, he didn't care. Boots glanced at me for the first time.

"How about this jerk-off?" he said.

I nodded at Hawk.

"I'm with him," I said.

"And you do what he says?" Boots asked me.

"I do."

Boots sort of snorted. He turned to the big Ukrainian.

"You down with this?" he said.

"Down?" Fadeyushka said.

"Learn the fucking language," Boots said. "Are you fucking okay with it."

Fadeyushka looked straight at Hawk for a time.

"For now," he said. "I am down."

Some seagulls hopped near the pavilion, looking for food. The wind blew a hamburger wrapper past them. Two of them flew up and lighted on it and tore at it and found no sustenance, and turned away.

"Remember something valuable," Boots said to Hawk. "Do not fuck with me."

Hawk seemed to smile a little.

"Long as you down with Tony," Hawk said. "You down with me."

Boots looked hard at Hawk for another moment, then turned and walked to the car. Fadeyushka followed him and the cops peeled off behind them. The rest of us stood as the procession pulled away, leaving us alone with the wind and the seagulls.

32

———•———

CECILE HAD a condominium in a gated enclosure on Cambridge Street, at the foot of Beacon Hill, right across from Mass General, so she could walk to work. She and Hawk had Susan and me to brunch there on the Sunday after we met with Boots and Tony.

The big loft space on the second floor had full-length arched windows, which Cecile had opened. The big ivory drapes that spilled out onto the floor were too heavy to blow in the spring breeze, but their edges fluttered a little while Hawk made each of us a Bloody Mary. Domestic.

We drank a couple of Bloody Marys, thus ensuring that I would nap when I got home. Cecile and Susan talked about their respective practices, and I shared occasional thoughts on sex and baseball, which, by and large, were all I had for thoughts. As usual, Hawk said little, though he seemed to enjoy listening. I had been reading a book about the human genome. We talked about that for a while. Cecile served us a variation of a dish my father called "shrimp wiggle": shrimp and peas in a cream sauce. Cecile served hers in pastry shells. My father didn't know what a pastry shell was, and with good reason. We had a little white wine with the shrimp. When I went to get a little more from the ice bucket, I noticed that Hawk's big .44 Mag was lying holstered on the sideboard among the wineglasses. The stainless-steel frame was good, but the brass edge of the cartridges that showed in the cylinder clashed with the cutlery.

We were nearly, and mercifully, through the shrimp wiggle when Cecile put her wineglass down suddenly and sat, staring at her plate. Sitting beside her, Hawk put his hand on her thigh. Her shoulders began to shake and then she looked up and there were tears running down her face. Hawk patted her thigh softly.

"This is so awful," Cecile said.

Her voice was shaky.

"We had a fight about this before you came."

She dabbed carefully at her eyes with her napkin. There were still tears.

"We sit here and eat and drink and make small talk," she said, and pointed at Hawk.

"And he was almost shot and killed and now he's going to kill other people, probably already has, to get even, or get killed trying to get even, and"—she pointed at me—"he's helping. And no one will tell me anything about it or explain it or even talk about it, so we sit here and chit-chat and gossip and pretend."

Hawk continued to pat her thigh. Otherwise it was as if he hadn't heard her.

"It's not pretend, Cecile," Susan said. "Because these men aren't like other men you know doesn't mean that they are simply different. Because they are engaged in life-and-death matters sometimes doesn't mean that they can't waste time other times talking about sex or baseball."

"It's not wasting time," I said.

Susan glared at me, but flickering at the edge of the glare was amusement.

"I could accept that," Cecile said, "maybe. If only somebody could explain to me what the hell they are doing and why."

"It's a terrible left-out feeling, isn't it," Susan said.

"I'm terrified. I'm horrified. I can't understand it. And the man who is supposed to love me won't even explain himself."

I know Susan heard "supposed to love me," and I knew she knew that it could mean more than one thing. But Susan was not a proponent of freelance shrinkage over drinks on a Sunday afternoon. Thank God!

"Maybe he can't explain it," Susan said.

"So let him say he can't explain it," Cecile said.

Susan was quiet. So was I. Hawk gently took his hand from Cecile's thigh and stood and walked to the sideboard. He picked up the holstered gun and turned and walked out the front door, and closed it gently behind him. All of us were quiet for a moment.

Then Cecile said, "Oh my God!" and began to cry. We were quiet while she cried. Finally she eased up and dabbed some more at her eyes with her napkin. Some of her eye makeup had run a little in the big cry.

"I'm sorry," she finally said.

"Loving Hawk is not easy work," I said.

"It seems easy for you."

"Apples and pears," I said.

Cecile tossed her chin at me. It was not completely affectionate.

"Does Spenser talk to you?" she said to Susan.

"I'm afraid he does," Susan said.

"And you understand him?"

"Yes."

"How do you stand it—the guns, the tough-guy stuff?"

"The relationship seems worth it," Susan said.

"And you can't change him?"

"He has changed," Susan said. "You should have seen him when we first met."

She smiled for a moment and looked at me.

"How did you do it?" Cecile said.

"I didn't. He did," Susan said.

Cecile looked at me aggressively, as if somehow Hawk were my fault.

"Is that right?"

"I learned things from her," I said. "I do, after all, love her."

The minute I said it I knew it was the perfect wrong thing.

"And Hawk doesn't love me?" Cecile said.

"He loves you better than anyone else I've ever seen him with," I said.

"Oh, goodie," Cecile said.

With Hawk unavailable, she was mad at me.

"Have you told Cecile about the time the Gray Man shot you?" Susan said to me.

"Some."

"He was almost killed. It took about a year to recover. Hawk and I took him to a place in Santa Barbara, and Hawk rehabbed him."

Cecile nodded.

"What did you do," Susan said, "when you were sufficiently rehabbed."

"I found him and put him in jail."

"Did he stay in jail?"

"No, we made a deal; he solved a case for me, DA let him go."

"Did you mind?" Susan said.

"That he got let go? No. We were even anyway."

Susan looked at Cecile as if they both had a secret.

"Why did you track him down?" Susan said.

"I can't let somebody shoot me and get away with it."

"Why?"

"Very bad for business," I said.

"Any other reasons?"

"I needed him to solve the case."

"Did the police help you find him?"

"No."

"Why not?"

"I needed to do it myself."

Susan didn't say anything. She and Cecile shared their secret again. I sipped a little white wine. Some sort of mediocre Chardonnay. I didn't like it much, but any port in a storm. Then I saw it: where Susan had taken me, and why.

"I was afraid," I said to Cecile. "I was afraid of the Gray Man, and of dying, and of not seeing her again."

"Not seeing Susan," Cecile said.

"Yes. It was intolerable. I can't do what I do, or be who I am, if I'm afraid."

"So you had to get back up and ride the horse again," Cecile said.

"Yes."

Cecile was silent, looking at me and at Susan.

"He's afraid," she said finally. "Like you were."

Susan nodded.

"And he can't say it."

"He may not even know it," Susan said.

"He knows," I said.

Susan nodded. Cecile drank some of her wine. She didn't seem to notice it was mediocre.

"But"—Cecile spoke slowly as if she were watching the sun rise gradually—"either way, he has to prove that they can't kill him."

"Yes," I said.

"And you will help Hawk do that," she said to me.

"Yes."

Cecile looked at Susan.

"And you'll let him do that?" she said.

"Wrong word," Susan said. "I know why he is helping, and I don't try to stop him."

"Because?"

"Because I love him," Susan said, "and not someone I might make him into, if I could, which I can't."

"What if you could make me into Brad Pitt?" I said.

"That would be different," Susan said.

33

BROCK RIMBAUD ran his operation out of a storefront at number five Naugus Street, which was a street just wider than an alley and not as long. There were five buildings on the street, all flat-roofed three-decker tenements, where the kitchens probably still smelled of kerosene. The storefront was on the first floor of the second three-decker in. The building was sided in yellowish asphalt shingles, with sagging porches across the face of the second and third floors. There were clotheslines in use on both porches.

On the plate-glass window that formed the front of Rimbaud's digs on the first floor was a black-letter sign that read RIMBAUD ENTERPRISES. The black lettering was edged with gold. Nicely coherent with the neighborhood.

"You know what we're going to do here?" I said to Hawk.

"Talk with the Brockster," Hawk said.

"Aside from the pure pleasure of it," I said. "What are we trying to accomplish?"

"Hell," Hawk said, "you ought to know how this works. Start in, poke around, talk to people, ask questions, see what happens? I learned it from you all these years."

"It's known in forensic circles as the Spenser method," I said.

"Also known as *I don't have any idea what the fuck I'm doing,*" Hawk said.

"Also known as that," I said. "Nice to know you've been paying attention."

"Learning from the master," Hawk said.

I took my gun in its clip-on holster off my hip and put it on under my blazer in front where I could get at it easily while sitting down. I knew Hawk had a shoulder rig. We got out of the car and walked to Rimbaud's office.

"What the fuck do you want," Rimbaud said when we went in.

He was sitting in a high-backed red leather swivel chair behind a gray metal desk. There was a pigskin leather humidor on the desk, and a phone, and a nine-millimeter handgun.

"See," Hawk said, "he remember us."

"And fondly," I said.

Rimbaud didn't seem to know what else to say, so he gave us a mean look. There were two skinny black Hispanic men in the room with him each wearing a colorful long-sleeved shirt unbuttoned over a ribbed undershirt—one gray, one white. Their shirttails were out, and the cuffs were rolled back over their slim forearms. They each gave us a mean look.

"Mind if we sit?" Hawk said.

Rimbaud nodded toward a couple of straight chairs near his desk. He was wearing a white shirt with the top three buttons undone and the cuffs turned loosely back over his forearms. We sat. The room was empty except for the desk and a few chairs. On a back wall was the only ornamentation, a large movie poster of Al Pacino in *Scarface*. Hawk smiled at Brock. I smiled at Brock.

Brock said, "So?"

"Come by to see how you doing with Boots," Hawk said.

"Boots who?" Rimbaud said.

He was absently fondling the gun on his desk.

"Brock," Hawk said. "Mind if I call you Brock?"

Rimbaud rolled his hand in a small, impatient circle.

"Brock," Hawk said again. "You know and we know that you up here trying to move in on Boots Podolak's operation."

"And what's that?" Rimbaud said.

"Marshport," Hawk said.

Rimbaud looked at his two companions and rolled his eyes. They both laughed. One of them brushed his open shirt away from his belt so we could see the gun he wore on his left side, butt forward.

"Look at that," I said to Rimbaud. "Just like your gun. You get a buy on them. You know, buy two, get one free?"

"You got something on your mind," Rimbaud said, "or you just come here to crack wise?"

Hawk grinned and looked at me.

"You doing that again?" he said.

"Cracking wise is my game," I said.

Hawk nodded and turned back to Rimbaud.

"You want Podolak out of business," Hawk said. "So do we. I'm looking to see if we can help each other."

"I don't need no help," Rimbaud said.

"Sure you do," I said. "Your father-in-law didn't have a deal with Boots to let you operate up here, you'd be, ah, cracking wise with the fishes."

Hawk smiled.

"Tony?" Rimbaud said.

Hawk said, "Un-huh."

Rimbaud's face flushed.

"Tony ain't got no deal with Boots," he said. "I'm in here because Boots isn't tough enough to keep me out."

Hawk smiled. He had a great smile. Even white teeth in

his smooth, black countenance. The smile was bright and clean and handsome . . . entirely devoid of feeling.

"Son," Hawk said, "Boots had a parakeet, the parakeet would be tough enough to keep you out."

"You think so?" Rimbaud said.

The flush on his face was bright now and widespread. His voice had gone up an octave. He picked up the gun and pointed it at Hawk. The minute Rimbaud raised his gun, the other two men took out theirs.

"You think maybe I'm not tough enough," Rimbaud said, "to shoot your fucking ass right now?"

I hadn't been shot as recently as Hawk. But it isn't something you forget. Funny thing was, I never thought of the bullets hitting me. I thought of the hospital, of the lights and tubes and sounds. I remembered the weakness, the craziness, the paranoid delusions. I thought of the smells. It didn't control me; I was always able to put it away, but the memory lurked in my cell structure.

Slowly Hawk put one foot up on the edge of Rimbaud's desk. He smiled and tilted his chair back so that he was rocking gently on the back legs. He held the smile and said nothing as he rocked.

"Nothing to say, Big Mouth?" Rimbaud said.

"You need an army to shoot it out with Boots," Hawk said. "And I don't think you got one."

"We can keep nibbling at his business until we got it all," Rimbaud said.

"You nibble enough to threaten him and the deal with Tony won't hold," Hawk said.

"I don't know nothing about no deal," Rimbaud said. "He gives us trouble and we'll take him out. I'll take him out, me, personal."

Hawk nodded.

"And another guy will take over who won't want you nibbling at the business, either."

Rimbaud didn't say anything, a rare moment of relief.

"Brock," I said. "He's got an army; you got a squad, maybe. Tony may help you for a while, but if it comes down to it, he's not going to go full-bore to the mattresses twenty-five miles from his own turf. My guess is he'd throw you to the Ukrainians and take his daughter home."

Rimbaud said, "She ain't going noplace."

Neither Hawk nor I said anything. Rimbaud sat, trying to think. The gun was still raised, but I think he'd forgotten it. After a while he put it down. His two pals put theirs away. Hawk continued to rock.

"You got a plan?" Rimbaud said.

"Nope, we sort of looking for one," Hawk said.

"I got ten men," Rimbaud said. He nodded at the other two. "Nuncio and Jaime, and eight other guys. I make eleven."

"You know how many Boots has got?" Hawk said.

"I don't know. Fuck him. I don't even care."

"Better if you knew," Hawk said. "Why here?"

"You mean why try to take over Marshport?"

"Yeah."

"I'm looking for a place to do business, see. And I figure to do it smart. So I look for a place ready to blow up, you know? And here it is, Marshport, a black and Latin city run by a bunch of white Bohunks, like, ah, you know, like ripe and ready."

"Except there's a lot of the Bohunks," I said, "and all of them are tougher than Donald Trump's agent."

"I'm white," Rimbaud said. "But only on the outside. I mean, I grew up black. I'm like black inside. I know about black. I can bring these people around."

"Okay, bro," Hawk said. "You keep on doing what you're doing and we'll check in with you once in a while, let you know what we're doing."

"What are you doing now?" Rimbaud said.

He didn't sound black inside.

"Collecting data," Hawk said.

"That's all?"

"Un-huh."

"What you going to do when you get enough data?" Rimbaud said.

"Depend on what the data tell us," Hawk said. "Tha's why we gathers it."

Rimbaud leaned back in his chair.

"I guess we're after the same thing," he said. He took a cigar from the leather humidor and began to trim the end with a small penknife.

Expansive.

Hawk nodded.

"Give him a card," Hawk said to me, "case he care to call us."

"Sure," I said.

I stood, took a card from my card case, and bent over the desk to put it in front of Rimbaud. Rimbaud was too cool to look at it while we were there.

"I have anything," he said, "I'll let you know."

Hawk stood.

"Have a nice day, bro," Hawk said.

Then we turned and went out the front door.

"Bro?" I said as we walked across the street.

"You heard him," Hawk said. "He say he black inside."

"Rimbaud isn't anything inside," I said.

Hawk grinned.

"You honkies always badmouth a brother," he said.

34

———•———

SUSAN SAT with Hawk and me at the downstairs bar in a restaurant Susan liked, called Upstairs on the Square.

"Do you guys have any plan at all?" she said.

Hawk smiled at her.

"Was thinking of getting drunk," he said. "First time since I got shot."

"I've never seen you drunk," Susan said. "Do you get witty and elegant, like my honey does?"

"Never been that drunk," Hawk said.

In honor of the conversation, I took another swallow of my Blue Label and soda.

"Well," Susan said, "before you are, tell me a little more about Marshport."

Hawk's grin widened.

"You gonna help us?"

Susan had returned to drinking white wine. Her favorite was now Riesling. She drank a very small amount of it. We were at one end of the bar, sitting at the turn, with Susan between us.

"You think you have to be some sort of big ugly thug to think about things like this?" Susan said.

Hawk studied his champagne cocktail for a moment.

"Big handsome thug," Hawk said, without looking up.

"That's what I meant," Susan said. "As far as I can tell, you know what you want to do up there. But have no idea how to do it."

Hawk looked at me. I shrugged.

"You know how to do it?" I said.

"No," Hawk said. "You?"

"No."

I looked at Susan.

"Step right up, little lady," I said.

"What if I actually help you?" Susan said.

"Be humiliated," Hawk said. "But we work through it."

"All right," she said. "Bear with me, while I review."

The bar was crowded. There was a small space next to

Hawk, but no one crowded into it. An attractive woman stopped to speak to Susan. Susan introduced us. The woman's name was Chris Lannum.

"We do Pilates together," Susan said.

"The rest of us just struggle to keep up with Susan," Chris said.

She smiled and moved on toward her table. As she went she gave Hawk a fast appraisal. On the Cambridge bar scene, Hawk is somewhat atypical.

"You want to kill the Ukrainian men who shot Luther and his family."

"And me," Hawk said.

"And you wish to destroy the entire Ukrainian mob structure in Marshport. Root and branch, so to speak."

"So to speak," Hawk said.

"In addition," Susan said, "you wish to provide a lifetime of financial security for Luther's surviving child."

"Yes."

"Currently," Susan said, "you are in an uneasy alliance with Tony Marcus, who, on behalf of his daughter and son-in-law, is in an uneasy alliance with . . . what's that man's name?"

"Boots," I said. "Boots Podolak."

She nodded.

"Do you wish to kill Boots?" she said to Hawk.

"Yes."

"If you kill Boots, would you eliminate one candidate to fund the Gillespie boy's trust fund?"

"Yes," Hawk said.

"Is there any other source?" Susan said.

"Tony got jing," Hawk said.

"Would he or Podolak voluntarily invest it in the child?"

"No."

"You'll have to force it."

"Yes."

Susan paused to drink some wine. At her table across the room, Chris Lannum threw her head back and laughed at something. The room was quite amazing, with a vast, high ceiling, a fireplace, and elegantly over-the-top décor. Good place to drink. On the other hand, there were few bad places to drink.

"Some of what you want you can accomplish with relative ease, of course. We all know you can kill the Ukrainians and Podolak."

"Anybody can kill anybody," Hawk said.

"But that wouldn't eliminate the Marshport mob, and it wouldn't do anything for the Gillespie child."

"Name's Richard," Hawk said.

"Richard," Susan said.

She looked at me.

"The Gray Man is involved," she said.

I nodded.

"Do you trust him?"

"No."

"Do you think he's up to something?"

"I have no idea," I said. "It would just be foolish to trust him."

"And you have established contact," Susan said, "with the man married to Tony's daughter."

"Brock Rimbaud," I said. "Daughter's name is Jolene."

"Brock Rimbaud is his real name?"

"Don't know," I said. "My guess would be he invented it. He's that kind of guy."

"And how can he help you?" Susan said.

"Don't know," Hawk said. "Just keep poking around, see if something flies out."

"And the police are no use to you," Susan said.

"No," Hawk said.

"This has to be you," Susan said.

"Maybe a few friends," Hawk said.

Susan nodded. She drank more Riesling.

"Of course you know I hate this whole enterprise," she said.

Hawk and I both nodded.

"But you'll do what you're going to do," she said, "so I might as well help as best I can." She paused. "I know far too much about shrinkage and life to try psychotherapy at the bar, drinking white wine."

"Oh, good," Hawk said.

Susan smiled.

"But you need to understand that you are in unfamiliar territory here. You have always in the past known what to do. It may have been a hard, dangerous thing. But you're good at that, and you alone had to accept the consequences of doing it or not doing it."

Hawk nodded at me.

"Ain't so different than him," he said.

"There are similarities," Susan said. "But here you have Cecile to think about, and Richard Gillespie, and Tony Marcus and his daughter are in here somewhere, and one thing you want to do contradicts another thing."

"I hate when it do that," Hawk said.

"And no one," Susan said. "Not even you, can go through being shot and nearly dying and spending days in the ICU and weeks in the hospital without being affected. You're smart enough to know that."

Hawk and I looked at each other. It had happened to both of us and we both knew she was right . . . about both of us.

"So, how that affect my plans?" Hawk said.

"More than anything, it makes it harder for you to have one. For maybe the first time in your, ah, professional life, you are being pushed by emotion."

"Spenser ain't got no plan, either," Hawk said. "He ain't being pushed by emotion."

"But he won't impose. You know him nearly as well as I do. He will stay with you, let you run it, go where you want to go."

Hawk nodded.

"He do that," Hawk said.

"He do that with me too," Susan said. "It drives me fucking crazy."

"Gee," I said, "I was liking it better when we were talking about Hawk's problems."

Susan smiled.

"Of course," she said. "And it's very decent to be that way, but sometimes it's not useful. You need to know what you know, what you don't know, and what you have to know. And you need to have it in mind. You need to know what part of what you want to do can be done now, and what needs to wait, and what it needs to wait for. Is there anything you don't understand in this situation? Anything missing?"

I drank some scotch. Susan looked at me. Hawk looked at me. The bartender looked at me. I gestured for another round. No one said anything. I looked at Chris Lannum over at her table, having a nice time. The bartender came with the fresh drinks. I finished my first scotch just in time.

"Okay," I said. "Thing's been bothering me from the moment his name popped up. Boots Podolak. He's nasty. But he's got no stature. And he's dumber than a candlepin."

"You wonder why he's the big boss in Marshport," Susan said.

"Yeah. Boss Tweed he ain't."

"You think maybe somebody proppin' him up?" Hawk said.

"Be something to find out," I said.

"I been so busy thinking 'bout killing him . . ."

"Be a place to start," I said.

"Would," Hawk said. "Might be nice to find out for sure what happened to that lawyer, Duda, that went to Miami."

"Would," I said. "Might be wise to talk with Rita Fiore, know what arrangement we could actually make for Luther's kid."

Hawk nodded and grinned at Susan.

"See, tole you we could help you," he said, "we put our mind to it."

Susan smiled back at him and put her hand on top of his.

"I'm very grateful," she said.

35

WE HAD DRINKS with Rita Fiore in the late afternoon at a table by the window in the Ritz Bar on Arlington Street. Rita's interest in Hawk was radiant, but she was in her professional mode and she kept it under control. She did manage to sit sideways in her chair for a while and stretch out her legs in such a manner that Hawk could admire them. Which he did. Me too.

"Sure," Rita said. "We can set up an escrow account for this kid and it can be funded by anybody that wants to."

"Confidential?" Hawk said.

"Sure."

"Who manages it?" Hawk said.

"I do criminal law," Rita said, and smiled, "so I'm at ease with you guys. But I don't do stocks and bonds. I'll have it managed by one of our stocks-and-bonds people."

"I want you," Hawk said.

"And I want you too, darlin'," Rita said. "But it's not in your best interest to have me manage the thing. I could lose money on insider trading. What I can do, though, is I'll godfather it. It will scare the hell out of the stocks-and-bonds people, and they'll give the account especially good service."

The waiter brought Rita a fresh martini. Up, with olives. The classic. No pink drinks or flavored vodka for Rita. An old-fashioned girl. She took a happy sip.

"This is unlike you, Hawk," Rita said.

"Sometimes I jess let it all go," he said.

"Mr. Soft Heart, here"—Rita nodded toward me—"I'd expect it. But you?"

"Boy's an orphan," Hawk said.

"You have something to do with that?" Rita said.

"I was supposed to protect his father," Hawk said.

"Ah," Rita said. "When you got shot."

"You keepin' track," Hawk said.

"I am a great track keeper," she said. "And you're doubly interesting; great potential as a sex partner, and very likely to need a first-rate criminal lawyer."

"One-stop shopping," Hawk said.

"And top of the line," Rita said.

Hawk grinned.

"Keep it in mind," he said.

"You feel responsible for this little boy?" Rita said.

"Yes."

"What could you have done?"

"Kept his father from getting killed."

"Hell, Hawk," Rita said. She leaned forward slightly, as if, for the moment, she seemed to have forgotten her libido. "They shot you in the back; how can it be your fault?"

"I ain't supposed to get shot in the back."

"For crissake," Rita said. "You're a man, like other men. You can be hurt. You can be killed."

"Ain't supposed to be like other men," Hawk said.

Rita looked at him for a moment.

"Jesus," she said. "It must be hard being you."

Hawk was quiet for a time, then he smiled at her, which was nearly always a startling sight.

"Worth it, though," he said.

36

LOCK OBERS was shiny and good under new ownership after some years of decline. Now it was once again the place for power lunches, which I must have been having, because I was there, eating with the Special Agent in Charge of the Boston FBI office.

His name was Nathan Epstein. He was thin and balding, with round, dark-rimmed glasses and pale skin. He didn't look like an FBI agent. In fact, he didn't look like much of anything. But he was smart, and I had heard that he knew how to shoot.

"Why are you interested in Boots Podolak," he said.

"You don't need to know," I said.

Epstein nodded.

"'Course I don't," he said. "I don't need to know anything you know. And you don't need to know anything I know."

Epstein took a forkful of limestone lettuce and stuffed it in his mouth and chewed vigorously. I looked at my lobster stew for a moment.

"Do I hear a quid pro quo being asserted?" I said.

Epstein chewed his lettuce and swallowed it.

"You do," he said.

I nodded.

"We want to take him down," I said.

"We?"

"Me and a friend of mine."

"Friend who was almost shot to death last year?"

"Yes."

"Blames Boots?"

"We know Boots had something to do with it," I said. "You been keeping tabs on us?"

Epstein grinned at me.

"We don't like Boots, either," he said.

"You've been keeping tabs on Boots," I said.

Epstein pointed at me in affirmation.

"And up we popped," I said.

"You and Hawk," Epstein said.

"So what can you tell me?"

"You first," he said.

"Off the record," I said.

"You expect to engage in criminal activity in this venture?" Epstein said.

"Just being careful," I said. "It is possible that Hawk might, unknowingly, violate a federal statute."

"I work for the federal government," Epstein said. "I am not unfamiliar with criminal activity."

"Good point," I said. "So, off the record?"

Epstein nodded, and chewed some more lettuce. I told him the part about Hawk and the Ukrainians, and Hawk getting shot, and us dismantling Boots's operation to even things up. I trusted Epstein. I'd worked with him before. I told him about Tony Marcus and Brock Rimbaud, and the adventures we'd had in Marshport. Epstein listened silently while he ate his salad.

"I heard there was a Ukrainian guy got himself popped over on Blue Hill Ave a while ago."

"People are often popped on Blue Hill Ave," I said.

"Most of them aren't Ukrainian."

"Well," I said. "Not all of them, certainly."

"You and Hawk in on that?"

I smiled.

"I'll take that as a yes," Epstein said.

The waiter brought him some broiled scallops. Epstein started on them at once. I continued with my lobster stew.

"You talk to Ives at all?" Epstein said.

"Ives?"

"Yeah. You talk with him?"

"Why would I talk with Ives?" I said.

Epstein shrugged.

"I know you know him," Epstein said. "Got the Ukrainian connection. Ives is on the foreign side of things."

"You been in touch with Ives," I said.

"Yes."

"So you know I talked with him, because he told you."

Epstein stabbed a scallop with his fork and disposed of it.

"Well, since you put it that way," he said. "Yes."

"We needed a tough guy that spoke Ukrainian," I said. "I figured Ives would be a better source than Berlitz."

"He gave you the Gray Man," Epstein said between scallops.

I sat back and put my spoon down.

"Rugar," I said.

"His name changes more often than his appearance," Epstein said. "I always call him the Gray Man."

"He speaks Ukrainian," I said.

"He speaks a lot of things," Epstein said.

I nodded. Epstein finished his scallops.

"They still got Indian pudding here?" he said.

"I think so."

"Love Indian pudding," he said.

"Isn't that nice," I said.

The waiter cleared the table. Epstein ordered Indian pudding with ice cream. I had coffee. Men in suits and women in skirts came in and went out. The huge polished urns behind the service counter gleamed. The window next to us looked out on Winter Place, which was far too small an alley to live up to its name. Cold spring rain made all the surfaces in Winter Place gleam pleasantly. The waiter came back with coffee and Indian pudding. A scoop of vanilla ice cream sat on top of the pudding. Epstein looked at it happily.

"You don't like Indian pudding?" he said to me.

"I do. But not right now."

"Guy your size," Epstein said. "You don't eat enough."

I nodded. Epstein poked the ice cream with a spoon.

"Too hard," he said, and put the spoon down. "Give it a little time."

Epstein sat back a little and sipped some coffee. He was in no hurry. He was never in any hurry. He had all the time he needed. He'd get to where he was going when he needed to. I was getting tired of waiting for him. Which I knew was also a tactic. What would I say to get him talking? When in doubt, go with what you do best. I shut up. Epstein tested his Indian pudding again, nodded to himself, and took a bite.

"Boots Podolak took over the business of running Marshport," he said, "from his father, whose name was Holovka Podolak, who came to Marshport after a long time in the

Russian mob and scratched out a living in the Ukrainian neighborhood, known as Strashnyy, which is, by the way, Ukrainian for 'horrible.' Holovka scratched so good and so often that eventually, in the late seventies, he took the city away from the Micks, who had taken it away from the Yankees."

"It's mostly black Hispanic now," I said.

"It's been black Hispanic for forty years," Epstein said. "But not at the top."

"Gee," I said.

"Holovka was mean and smart and had a lot of, ah, Eurasian connections," Epstein said.

He shoveled in some more pudding.

"And when he passed it on to Boots, the whole thing should have fallen apart, because Boots is a poster child for gene pool dilution, but Holovka had made an alliance with an Afghani warlord."

"In Afghanistan?" I said.

"You think there are Afghani warlords hanging around pool halls in Marshport?" Epstein said. "Yes, an Afghanistan-based Afghani warlord."

He grinned and went back to his Indian pudding. I waited, drinking my coffee, watching him finish it off. I wondered if the name was politically correct. Shouldn't it be Native American pudding?

"Opium," I said.

Epstein nodded his head in a congratulatory way.

"Doesn't take you long," he said. "Podolak is the exclusive East Coast, U.S.A. distributorship for an Afghani warlord named Haji Haroon."

"Where'd the connection with Holovka come from?" I said.

"We don't know. We're guessing his father established it before he came to Marshport. We think he spent time there, maybe in his Russian mob days. The Soviets were there for a long time."

"And didn't it work out good for them," I said.

Epstein smiled.

"Opium's kind of bulky," I said.

"Too bulky for distant export like this," Epstein said.

"So Haji ships heroin."

"Exactly right," Epstein said. "And nicely alliterative."

"Does Haji supply, ah, management expertise?"

"He does."

"Afghani?"

Epstein shrugged.

"We don't know," he said.

"But you know there is somebody keeping an eye on Boots."

"We are convinced. Boots couldn't do this alone. And the Afghans don't trust members of another tribe, let alone some American of Ukrainian descent ten thousand miles away."

"So there's somebody."

"There has to be."

"So the Ukrainians are muscle."

"Yes."

"And there's an Afghani supervisor."

"Has to be," Epstein said.

"But we don't know who or where."

"Exactly," Epstein said.

I was quiet for a minute, watching Epstein enjoy his lunch.

"With that kind of setup," I said, "why is Boots trying to move into other turf?"

"We wondered about that, too," Epstein said. "Now that I know about the Marcus family involvement, I'd say there are two probable reasons. One is: The opportunity presented itself when Tony wanted to help his son-in-law."

"And number two," I said. "Boots is stupider than a ball-peen hammer."

"Indeed," Epstein said.

"So what about the supervisor?"

"Maybe he's not so smart, either?" Epstein said.

"Or maybe," I said, "since the fix was in with Tony, they figured it was free money."

"Everyone likes free money," Epstein said.

"So," I said. "I see your interest. What's up with Ives?"

"We talk to one another more since nine-eleven."

"Wise," I said. "But I was asking what Ives's interest is."

"You'll probably need to ask him," Epstein said.

"I probably will."

Epstein drank the last of his coffee, looked sadly at the empty pudding dish, and pushed his chair back.

"Thanks for lunch," he said.

"I gather I'm paying?"

"How nice of you to offer," he said.

"I'm very patriotic," I said.

37

___·___

WE HAD a little meeting to discuss plans. Five of us.
Tony wanted one of his people on the scene, so he gave us
Leonard. I wanted somebody to watch my back while I was
watching Hawk's back, so I invited Vinnie Morris, who
could shoot the smell off a skunk at one hundred yards. And
we needed a Ukrainian speaker, so Rugar, whose name was
now something else, but he wouldn't tell us what, had
agreed to be there.

Hawk arrived at my office before anyone else. I had not
talked with him yet about my discussion with Epstein. I

wanted first to discuss it with Ives. But I had a sense that the Gray Man might be more, or less, than he seemed to be.

"There's not a lot of time before the others get here," I said to Hawk. "But don't say any more than you have to in front of the Gray Man."

"Like I usually say more than I have to in front of anybody?" Hawk said.

"Gray Man's interests may not fully coincide with ours," I said.

"I'm shocked," Hawk said.

Vinnie came in with Leonard.

"You got coffee?" Vinnie said.

"I'm making it," I said.

And began to.

"Sinkers?" Vinnie said.

I reached behind my desk and plonked a box of Dunkin' Donuts on my blotter. Vinnie opened the top and looked in and nodded as if I had vindicated myself again.

"Nice working with you," Vinnie said.

He sat beside Leonard on the couch across the far wall and waited for the coffee to brew. My office door opened again and the Gray Man came in carefully, wearing his showy trademark outfit of gray suit, tie, shirt, hair, and eyes. There was nothing special about my office. I knew the Gray Man entered everywhere carefully. He sat on a straight chair to the left of my desk, turning the chair so that his back was not to Vinnie or Leonard . . . or the door. The coffee brewed. We all had some. I put the donuts in the middle of my desk, and people helped themselves at will.

"Do you have any scones?" the Gray Man said.

I shook my head. The Gray Man had a moment of disapproval and then had a donut instead.

"So how many buttons we gotta push," Vinnie said, "to put these people out of business."

"Don't know yet," Hawk said. "Tony got any thoughts, Leonard?"

"No," Leonard said pleasantly.

He was wearing a light-blue suit with a lavender shirt and tie. The tie probably cost more than my full attire. His neck was muscular above the Windsor collar.

"Spenser?" Hawk said.

"The town is locked up tight," I said. "There's a newspaper, the Marshport *Call*. Boots owns it. There's a radio station, WMAR, which is owned by a woman named Lucille Davidoff. Lucille is Boots's sister. Boots has run unopposed in the last four mayoral elections. There is no police union, the cops belong to Boots. Everywhere Boots goes, some Marshport cops go with him. The inner circle is Ukrainian, most of them Ukrainian nationals."

"Which be where Mr. Gray Man be useful," Hawk said.

The Gray Man looked vaguely self-effacing. It was a little hard to tell what he was thinking without close observation. His expression rarely changed.

"We could pop them one at a time," Vinnie said.

"We gonna pull the whole thing down," Hawk said. "We may pop some and we may pop them all, and we may do it one at a time, and we may do it all at once. But we gonna pull it down and they gonna know it was me that done it and they gonna know why and they gonna leave behind a trust fund for Luther Gillespie's kid."

"You have a plan?" I said.

"I just gave you the plan."

"Besides that," I said.

"No."

"Swell," I said. "How about we spray-paint UKRAINIANS SUCK on prominent buildings?"

"If I may," the Gray Man said. "The strategy is sound—take over the city. What we need are"—he glanced at me and smiled faintly—"additional tactics to accomplish the strategy."

The Gray Man's smile was as substantial as a wisp of fog on a windy night.

"I understand that they are short at least two Ukrainians," he said.

"They shot one," Hawk said, "and I shot one."

"Perhaps they would welcome a replacement."

"You?"

"Perhaps I could join them," the Gray Man said.

"You Ukrainian," Hawk said.

"I am a citizen of the world," the Gray Man said. "I am fluent in Ukrainian."

"What do we do for a translator?" I said.

"One does not necessarily preclude the other."

"Why?" I said.

"Why am I willing to help you?"

"Yeah."

"I tried to kill you and almost succeeded. Maybe it puts me in your debt."

"You think that's it?" I said.

"Possibly."

"You are a strange dude."

Again, the wispy, short-lived smile.

"We are all strange dudes," he said. "In what we do, there are no rules. We have to make some up for ourselves."

"Can you get in there?" Hawk said.

"Yes."

"Sure?"

"I have lived a various if desperate life," the Gray Man said. "I know a lot of people . . . and a lot of tricks."

Hawk nodded. The Gray Man looked carefully at Leonard.

"I commend you on your suit," he said.

Leonard nodded.

"I too like clothes."

Leonard nodded again. He carried a faint scent of sandal-wood.

"You work for Tony Marcus."

Leonard nodded.

"You are a neutral observer?" the Gray Man said.

Leonard shook his head.

"Then you are with us?"

"As long as Tony is," Leonard said.

The Gray Man nodded.

"Tony is changeable," I said.

"I have heard that," the Gray Man said.

Leonard remained within himself. For all I could tell, he was thinking about Stagger Lee and trying to remember the song lyrics. Vinnie had earphones in and was listening to his iPod. I drank some coffee. The Gray Man was right. We were all strange dudes.

Hawk looked at me. I shrugged.

"I don't see no reason you shouldn't get inside Boots's operation, if you can," Hawk said to the Gray Man.

"It may take some time," the Gray Man said.

"We got some time," Hawk said.

He looked at Vinnie.

"You the only one these people ain't seen," he said.

"Their loss," Vinnie said.

"Maybe you can hang out in Marshport," Hawk said. "In amongst the criminal element where you be right at home."

"I ain't no criminal," Vinnie said. "I'm a shooter. People hire me are criminals."

"See what you can see," Hawk said.

Vinnie was on his feet, selecting another donut from the box.

"Sure," he said.

"Bro," Hawk said to Leonard, "what you planning on doing."

"Stand by," Leonard said. "You need me, you holler."

"Might make sense if you hung around, kept an eye on Brock Rimbaud," Hawk said.

"He's so annoying," I said. "It's like a matter of moments before somebody can't stand it anymore."

Leonard smiled.

"I can do that," he said.

"You see anything interesting, you can let us know," Hawk said. "Balloon goes up, we let you know."

"Soon as we find a balloon," I said.

38

WHEN HAWK and I came down the long escalator from the second level, Ives was sitting on a circular bench near Bloomingdale's, on the first floor of the Chestnut Hill Mall, eating roasted cashews from a small bag.

"Ah," he said when we reached him, "the Nubian warrior."

"My people from Natal," Hawk said. "Ah is of Zulu extraction."

Ives smiled vaguely.

"Cashew?" he said.

I took a couple; they were still warm. Hawk shook his head.

"Spenser say you might be more interested in Boots Podolak than you letting on," Hawk said.

"Oh?"

"Say maybe you not as helpful as you seem," Hawk said. "Giving us the Gray Man."

"I didn't actually give him to you," Ives said.

His eyes were following a young woman in high heels and a short skirt who was heading down the mall toward Filene's.

"Lochinvar came to me, you'll recall, looking for a translator. The Gray Man seemed suitable."

"He work for you?" Hawk said.

Ives was wearing a tan summer suit with a blue oxford shirt and a green-and-blue striped tie. A snap-brimmed straw hat tilted forward over his narrow forehead. The wide hatband matched his tie. He studied the young woman for a moment as she receded down the mall. He ate a couple more cashews and offered me some. I shook my head.

"Currently?" Ives said. "He does."

"So what's he doing for us?" Hawk said.

"I assume he's helping you translate."

"And what's he doing for you?"

The young woman went into Filene's. Ives shook his head slightly in sorrow.

"Oh, my," Ives said. "Tight young ass."

Hawk didn't say anything.

"All ass is good," Ives said. "But these young housewives with their personal trainers . . . visions of sugarplums."

I said, "We're after the same thing, Ives."

"Tight young ass?"

"Besides that," I said. "You want something from Boots Podolak, and since officially you are supposed to work on foreign stuff only, you want something that has to do with the Afghan connection."

"Afghan connection?"

"You know he's got an Afghan connection, and I know you know it, and now you know I know it."

"I've always admired your ability, Lochinvar, to construct and speak complicated sentences without confusion."

"Yeah, it's special, isn't it?" I said.

"You know we after Boots," Hawk said.

Ives nodded.

"And you put the Gray Man in with us to see what we up to," Hawk said. "You didn't plan it that way maybe, but when Spenser come to you for translator help, there it was."

"Sometimes you have to let the game come to you," Ives said.

"Whassup," Hawk said. "With the game?"

"You show me yours," Ives said, "I'll show you mine."

Hawk looked at me.

"How much you tell him?"

"Just that I needed a tough guy who could speak Ukrainian. He knows it's about you getting shot."

"Or something," Hawk said.

I nodded.

"We trust him?" Hawk said.

"No," I said.

Ives smiled in self-deprecation and ate the last of his cashews.

"But I think you can tell him about this. He doesn't care who killed who?"

"Whom?" Ives said.

"Okay," Hawk said. "Got hired to protect a bookie named Luther Gillespie . . ." He told it all, without emotion, without slant, as if he were giving somebody directions to Anaheim. Ives listened without any expression. As he listened, he got a meerschaum pipe out of his coat pocket and filled it from an old-fashioned oilskin fold-over tobacco pouch, and lit it with a Zippo. The pipe tobacco smelled sweet.

When Hawk finished, Ives contemplated his pipe smoke for a time and then said, "So you are going to destroy his entire enterprise to get even."

"Ah'm going to destroy his entire enterprise," Hawk said.

"And Lochinvar?"

"What are friends for," I said.

Ives nodded. He glanced aimlessly around the mall. There were enough shoppers so that it was not discouraging. But it was an upscale mall, and it was rarely jammed on a weekday morning.

"Do you know what the Gray Man is currently calling himself?" Ives said. "Kodi McKean."

"C-O-D-Y?" I said.

Ives shook his head and spelled it.

"His cover name, when he needs to reach me, is the Kodiak Kid."

"The Kodiak Kid," I said.

"He finds it amusing," Ives said.

Ives blew a smoke ring. I waited. Hawk had enough dealings with Ives to know that waiting was part of the dance. He waited, too.

"As you clearly know, Mr. Podolak is the farthest eastern outpost of a criminal enterprise with its roots in Afghanistan, under the entrepreneurial direction of an Afghani named Haji Haroon. Mr. Haroon is what the press would describe as a warlord. I find the phrase a little too Kiplingesque."

"What would be your phrase?" I said.

"Haji Haroon is an independent ruler of a collection of his own tribesmen in Afghanistan," Ives said. "He has no allegiance beyond that. If asked his nationality, he would specify the tribe."

"Which is?"

"Alaza."

"Big tribe?" Hawk said.

"No, but cohesive and very vigorous on its own behalf. The Russians were terrified of them."

"So why do you care?" Hawk said.

"Well, of course, our government is opposed to heroin."

"Good to take a position," Hawk said.

"Yes," Ives said, watching the smoke drift up from his

pipe in a small spiral. "We're clear on that. And, further, we believe that some of the profits from the heroin trade are used in support of terrorism."

"By Mr. Haroon."

"We believe so," Ives said.

"Be good to know who the supervisor is," Hawk said.

"He is the key figure. We surmise, though we as yet don't know, that the skag goes to Podolak through him, and the money goes back to Haroon through him. He's the valve, so to speak, in the pipe. It would be satisfyingly disruptive to the system if he could be turned off."

"And why us?" I said.

Ives smiled.

"Because you're here," he said. "You are already involved."

He took the pipe out of his mouth and set it down in a big glass ashtray, with the stem carefully clear of the rim.

"And," he said, "in truth you are not just anybody. Nothing seems to frighten you, or at least frighten you sufficiently to deter you. And you are immensely formidable."

"Formidable," I said to Hawk.

"Immensely," Hawk said.

"I am hopeful that the Kodiak Kid can sufficiently ingratiate himself with Podolak and friends, that, perhaps, he can find the supervisor."

"And?"

Another young woman walked past us, wearing tight lowrider pants and a cropped T-shirt that stopped several inches shy of the pants. She had a small blue-and-red tattoo in the small of her back. Ives studied the tattoo for a while as the woman passed us toward Bloomingdale's. Then he turned back to us and smiled and made a sharp gesture with his hand and wrist as if he was turning off a valve.

39

THE EARLY SPRING weather was pretty good, so Hawk and I sat with the Gray Man on a set of stairs to one side of the brick wasteland that surrounded Boston City Hall.

"The Kodiak Kid?" I said to the Gray Man.

His face moved faintly as if to smile.

"It seems so American," the Gray Man said.

"And now that you're working for us," I said.

"Yes," the Gray Man said. "I wish to be totally American."

"Any progress?" Hawk said.

"I have made contact with the Ukrainian Janissaries. Monday I meet Podolak."

"Quick," I said.

"Strangers in a strange land," the Gray Man said, "like people who speak their language."

Hawk nodded.

"You know," I said, "it's still bothering me that Boots, given the setup he's got now with the Afghanis, would mess around with Tony Marcus's turf. Son-in-law or no."

"It is a very stupid thing to do," the Gray Man said.

"And I can't believe his keeper would approve."

"The Afghan supervisor," the Gray Man said, "could not be so stupid."

I scanned the plaza. At the moment, we were the only living things in sight. When they built the new city hall, some architect had doubtless conceived of this naked brick desert teeming with community. In the center of the desert was the slab-sided monolithic city hall that nestled into what had once been Scolly Square like a rhinoceros at a cotillion.

"Ain't a matter of smart," Hawk said. "Be pride."

"Boots?"

"Boots can't stand being told what to do by some West Asian wog," Hawk said.

"I don't think we call them wogs anymore," I said.

"Too Kiplingesque," Hawk said.

The Gray Man was staring at Hawk.

"Before the Afghani connection kicked in," I said, "he was the boss."

"Now the Afghani supervisor the boss," Hawk said.

"So along came this little deal that makes no sense, and Boots does it anyway."

"To prove that he could," the Gray Man said softly.

Hawk glanced at him.

"So," I said. "You think the supervisor knows?"

"My guess, he don't," Hawk said.

"Because if he did he'd shut down the heroin flow?"

"Yep."

"Which is why Boots doesn't have one of the Ukrainians cap him."

"If the Ukes all actually his," Hawk said.

"But he has his passive-aggressive drama," I said. *"I don't have to ask this guy for permission to do everything. This isn't even heroin business. It's mostly making book."*

"Passive-aggressive," Hawk said.

"I'm sleeping with a shrink," I said.

"I don't want to hear about it," Hawk said.

"You're quite sure about this," the Gray Man said.

Hawk nodded. The Gray Man looked at me. I nodded.

"All the more reason to find the supervisor," the Gray Man said.

"That sounds like a job for the Kodiak Kid," I said.

The Gray Man's smile was very faint.

"I know you find yourself amusing," he said. "But occasionally I would prefer to amuse myself."

"Hard to imagine," I said. "But your choice."

The Gray Man nodded.

"I will see what I can do," he said, and stood and walked away across the open empty plaza toward Tremont Street.

"Trust him?" Hawk said.

"No."

Hawk nodded.

"Trust Ives?" he said.

"No."

"How about Epstein?"

"He tells you he'll do something, I think he'll do it," I said.

"Would he lie to us?" Hawk said.

"Of course," I said.

"Don't trust Tony," Hawk said.

"And Leonard works for him."

"Obviously can't trust Boots," Hawk said, "or Brock Rimbaud."

"Obviously."

"'Cept for Vinnie," Hawk said, "it ain't a good assortment of trusty coconspirators."

"Seemed simpler," I said, "right after you got shot."

Hawk nodded.

"Kill a few Ukrainians," he said. "Go back about my business."

"Might have been that way if the guy on Blue Hill Ave had been scared to die," I said.

"Fucked up everything," Hawk said. "Now we're in business, for crissake, with the feds."

"My country right or wrong," I said, "but still my country."

"Yeah, sure," Hawk said. "Why doesn't Ives do some of this himself."

"He's got no domestic operation," I said, "officially."

"And the fucking bureau?" Hawk said.

"They're out pretty straight," I said. "Since nine-eleven. These guys live lives governed by funding. They are limited by statutes and regulations and shit."

"And we ain't," Hawk said.

"That's our charm," I said.

"You think anybody's had a tail on Boots? See if he leads to the supervisor?"

"Sure."

"So there be no point to us doing that," Hawk said.

"How would we even know if we did find him."

"You don't think he be wearing a head cloth and riding a camel?"

"I don't know if Afghan people ride camels," I said.

"We don't know shit," Hawk said.

"Often the case with us," I said.

"And we looking for somebody we may not recognize when we find him."

"Good point," I said.

"We could just kill everybody," Hawk said. "Let God sort 'em out."

"We could."

"And who funds the trust fund for Luther's kid."

"Maybe we could steal everybody's money before we killed them all," I said.

"Plus, you such a goddamned pantywaist," Hawk said, "you probably wouldn't even kill them all."

"I know," I said. "I know. I'm trying to improve."

"And we can't trust anybody we involved with, 'cept Vinnie."

"I know," I said. "I guess it's *Let us be true to one another, dear.*"

The plaza was always windy. Even on still days, the wind stirred the discard of urban life and blew it around on the bricks.

Hawk grinned.

"Don't call me *dear* in public," he said.

40

———•———

HENRY CIMOLI had taken the final upward leap in the transubstantiation of his boxing gym. He had added a Pilates studio to the Harbor Health Club. It was right next to the small boxing room he kept open as a paean to his past and a favor to Hawk and me. Susan came with us and took some Pilates training while Hawk and I lifted weights and repaired to the boxing room to teach the heavy bag a thing or two. Between rounds with the bag, I could watch through the window. She seemed flexible, strong, and tireless. She also seemed beautiful and smart, though my impressions may have been influenced by prior knowledge.

Showered, dressed, and rapturous with good health, Hawk and I waited in the lounge area for Susan. It took her longer to get rapturous. But when she emerged, she was. Her black hair gleamed. Her makeup was subtle and artistic. Her big eyes shone as they so often did with a sort of challenge. As if she was daring you to keep up with her.

"One of the ladies in the dressing room was complaining that a maintenance man had been caught peeping in."

Hawk glanced around the club at the women working out.

"Present company excluded," he said. "Why he want to do that?"

Susan smiled.

"I assumed it was me," she said.

"Had to be," Hawk said.

Outside, on Atlantic Ave, the dismantling of the elevated Central Artery was in full clamor. We walked a couple of blocks to the Boston Harbor Hotel and sat in the quiet lounge where we could look at the water.

"Brock and Jolene live right over there," Hawk said.

"Is that Tony Marcus's daughter and son-in-law?" Susan said.

"It is," I said. "Caesar and Cleopatra."

"Dumb and dumber," Hawk said.

"That too," I said.

The waitress brought beer for me and for Hawk. Susan had a vodka and tonic with a lime wedge.

"How is all that going?" she said. "Do I dare to ask?"

"Be my impression," Hawk said. "That there ain't much you don't dare."

"So how's it going?" she said.

"You want to tell her?"

"Sure," I said. "Don't hesitate to correct me if I get it wrong."

"Yeah," Hawk said. "You always so grateful, anyone corrects you."

"And gracious," Susan said.

"Shut up," I said, and told her everything I hadn't told her before.

By the time I got through, Hawk and I had each had a second beer, and Susan had already taken a swallow of her vodka and tonic.

"Well my God," Susan said. "You can't trust anyone."

"Vinnie probably okay," Hawk said.

"Except him. I mean, you don't know who is on your side, if anyone, or who is against you, if everyone."

"We noticed that," Hawk said. "We welcome any woman's intuition you want throw at us."

Susan gave Hawk a look.

"Oink," she said.

"Or reasoned analysis," I said.

Susan patted my hand.

"That's my good boy," she said.

Susan stared out the windows for a while at the harborscape.

―――

"Does anyone else in this mess trust anyone?" Susan said.

"No," I said.

"Brock whosis, or Tony, or Boots whatsisname, or Jolene, or the Ukrainians, or the Gray Man—I don't like the Gray Man being involved—anyone?"

"No."

One of the big cruise boats that took people around the harbor while they ate and drank began to ease out of its slip. Several seagulls flew angrily up as it moved.

"Perhaps you could make that work for you," Susan said.

"How," Hawk said.

"I have no idea yet. But there must be a way. There's a way to make everything work."

It was still daylight. But the cruise ship had its inside lights on. They shone through the wide windowed superstructure as the cruise ship moved away toward the mouth of the harbor, its wake spilling astern in smooth curls.

"No one better to figure out how to make use of the situation than you two," Susan said.

"True," Hawk said.

He was watching the boat. His hands rested motionless on the tabletop. I drank some beer and watched the boat, too.

After a while, I said, "We can think of something."

"Yes," Hawk said. "We can."

41

—●—

HAWK AND I spent the next two days in my office. We drank too much coffee. We ate too much Chinese food. We sat and we stood. We took turns standing and looking out the window at the women walking toward Boylston Street. I did a lot of scribbling on yellow legal-size pads.

"We gonna make sure that kid get his money," Hawk said every hour or so.

"We'll do that," I said every hour or so. "We just gotta figure out whose money he is going to get."

"We'll figure it out," Hawk said.

"We will," I said.

We both badly wanted a plan. I wanted one even more badly because Susan had suggested it, and I wanted it to work. In the middle of the afternoon on our second day of deliberations, the Gray Man came silently into the office and closed the door carefully behind him.

"I am in," he said, and sat down on the couch.

"In?" I said.

"The Boots Podolak organization," the Gray Man said. "I am now a member, and have already done them a service which ingratiates me."

"You kill somebody for them?" Hawk said.

The Gray Man nodded.

"They like that," Hawk said. "Nothing like scragging somebody, make people trust you."

"I know," the Gray Man said.

For a moment I felt it. A thing the Gray Man shared with Hawk.

"There's a balcony outside the window of Podolak's office in City Hall," the Gray Man said. "Somebody, some street soldier that's skimming, need to be punished, Podolak goes out on the balcony. Somebody hands him a .22 target pistol. Podolak sticks it in his belt. Down below, they shove the miscreant out of a cellar door, onto the street, and tell him to run for it. Podolak lets him get halfway up the block and draws, and just before he's going to make it to the corner, shoots him dead center between the shoulder blades at a good hundred yards. Miscreant goes down and Podolak shoots him several more times to be sure. He never misses, I'm told."

"He demonstrated this to you?" I said.

"Yes. It's supposed to impress me," the Gray Man said, "and, of course, to frighten me."

Hawk nodded. He had no expression.

"How far up you think you can get."

"Just below the Ukrainians," the Gray Man said.

"What happen if the Ukrainians go away?" Hawk said.

"I'd be just below Podolak."

"And if he went away," Hawk said.

"I believe I could replace him."

Hawk nodded. He walked to my desk and picked up my yellow pad and stared at the names and notes I had written and crossed out. I'm not sure he saw them.

"Boots doesn't suspect you," I said.

"No. Podolak is not a worldly man. I tell him stories of my adventures in countries he has never been to."

"They true?" I said.

The Gray Man smiled.

"Of course," he said. "Podolak has never traveled. He is very impressed."

"Neither worldly nor smart," I said. "Boots is living testimony to what simple meanness can achieve."

Hawk put the yellow pad down and looked out the window.

"And good aim," the Gray Man said. "But he is more than mean."

"More?"

"He enjoys cruelty and the power that comes from being able to inflict it."

"You know him that well already?" I said.

"I have known him most of my life," the Gray Man said.

Hawk turned back from the window.

"Okay," he said, "we in business."

"You have a plan?" I said.

"I do," Hawk said.

42

———•———

SUSAN AND PEARL and I were in bed together. I loved
Pearl, but my preference had always been a ménage à deux.

"At least she wasn't in here during," I said to Susan.

"It would not be decorous," Susan said.

"How about postcoital languor with a seventy-five-pound
hound on my chest. How decorous is that?"

"We don't wish to exclude her," Susan said.

"We don't?"

"No."

Pearl's head was on my chest, and her nose was perhaps an inch from mine. I gazed into her golden eyes. She gazed back.

"Not a single flicker of intelligence," I said.

"*Shhh,*" Susan said. "She believes she's smart."

"She's wrong," I said.

"Sometimes illusion is all we have," Susan said.

"Couldn't she settle for being beautiful," I said, "the way I have?"

"Apparently not," Susan said.

We were, all three of us, quiet then. The ceiling in Susan's bedroom was painted green. The walls were burgundy. Her sheets were sort of khaki-colored, and the pillowcases had a small gold trim. I reached around Pearl and held Susan's hand. She turned her head and smiled at me across the dog.

"Shall we have a big Sunday breakfast," she said, "while you tell me what's bothering you?"

"What makes you think something's bothering me?" I said.

Susan tilted her head a little.

She said, "You're dealing with a pro here, pal."

I let go of her hand and patted her belly.

"That's for sure," I said.

"I didn't mean that," Susan said.

I shrugged. Not an easy thing with a dog on your chest.

"What would you like for grub?" I said.

"Could we have apple fritters?"

"If you have the ingredients," I said.

"I have apples."

"Excellent start," I said.

"I don't know what else you need," she said.

"I'll check," I said, and struggled out from under Pearl and on to my feet.

"And put some pants on," Susan said. "I don't want the pity of my neighbors."

"They'd be green with envy," I said.

"Confidence is a good thing," Susan said. "But humor me."

I put on a pair of gym shorts that I kept at Susan's especially for postcoital leisurewear. She had managed to salvage just enough top sheet from Pearl to avoid being nude. I flexed at her.

"Dashing," she said.

I reached over and flipped the sheet off.

"Back at ya," I said.

I think she blushed very slightly, though I'm not sure. I turned and went to the kitchen.

She had apples and bananas and flour, and, amazingly, cornmeal and some oil. I made coffee and started assembling the fritters. I peeled the apples and skinned the bananas and sliced them and tossed each separately in some orange juice to keep them from turning brown. Then I mixed two small bowls of a flour-and-cornmeal batter, put the sliced apples into one and the bananas into the other. If there's plenitude, you may as well exploit it.

Susan came out of the bedroom with some lipgloss on and her hair brushed. She was wearing a short orange silk kimono-looking thing. I was prepared to eat at the counter, or standing up over the stove for that matter, but Susan had other plans. She put a tablecloth on the dining-room table and set it for two, complete with a glass vase of tulips that she brought in from the living room.

"Powdered sugar, honey, or maple syrup?" she said.

"I like syrup," I said.

"I like powdered sugar."

"Put out both," I said.

"God, you're decisive," she said.

I let the oil heat in the pot until it spattered when I sprinkled in water. Then I dropped the fritter batter in carefully, a few at a time, and cooked until I had stockpiled a significant serving of each. Susan drank coffee while I cooked.

When we settled in to eat, Susan said, "So, tell me about it."

"You shrinks are always so cocksure," I said.

"Nice word choice," Susan said. "In the current context."

I shrugged. Susan ate a bite of fritter.

"Wow," she said. "Banana, too?"

"Never a dull moment with Spenser," I said.

"Never," she said.

I had one each fritter with maple syrup and drank some coffee.

"Hawk's got a plan," I said.

Susan nodded and didn't speak.

"It's complicated, and requires people to react as we expect them to, and it will take some doing," I said. "But it's not a bad plan. It might work."

"Can you think of a better plan?" Susan said.

"I can't think of one as good," I said.

"Care to share?" Susan said.

I smiled.

"Sure," I said. "But you have to pay close attention."

"You'll help me with the hard stuff," Susan said.

"Count on me, little lady."

She didn't do anything while I told her but listen. She didn't drink coffee or eat or tap her fingertips together, or frown or smile or move. Susan could listen the ears off a brass monkey. When I got through, she was quiet for a moment.

Then she said, "If it's going to work, a number of people may have to be killed."

"Yes."

"Do you mind if they die?"

"Not too much. These aren't very good people."

"But you mind killing them."

"There are circumstances when I'd be comfortable with it," I said.

Susan nodded.

"But not these circumstances," she said.

"I don't think so," I said.

"You've killed people before," Susan said.

"I always felt I had to."

223

"But this seems like, what, serial assassination?" she said.

"Something like that."

"And if you walk away?" Susan said.

"I can't walk away."

Susan smiled slightly.

"I know," she said. "The question was rhetorical."

"The problem is not," I said.

I was being churlish and we both knew it, but Susan chose not to comment.

Instead, she smiled and said, "A fine mess you've got us into this time, Ollie."

I nodded.

"This doesn't bother Hawk," Susan said.

"No."

"Or the hideous Gray Man."

"I doubt that either of them has thought about it," I said.

"I wish the Gray Man weren't involved," Susan said.

I shrugged.

"The other day," I said, "I remarked that he was a strange dude, and he said, 'We are all strange dudes. In what we do, there are no rules. We have to make some up for ourselves.'"

"He always said you and he were alike," Susan said.

I nodded.

"Remember in San Francisco? When you and I were separated? And you killed a pimp? Just shot him."

"Yeah."

"Did you have to do that?"

"I had to find you," I said. "I couldn't stay around and protect those two whores from the trouble we got them into. When we left, the pimp would have killed them."

"So you had to kill him."

"Yes."

"To protect the whores from a jeopardy that you caused them."

"I was looking for you."

"So in a sense you did it for me?"

"I guess I thought so," I said.

"You don't lie to yourself," Susan said. "In your world, it had to be done."

I didn't say anything.

"Hawk has to do this," Susan said.

"He does."

"He and you," she said, "for your whole adulthoods, have been a certainty in each other's lives."

Susan ate the rest of her apple fritter, except for the piece she gave Pearl. She drank some coffee and put the cup down.

"In his life," she said, "you may be the only certainty."

"May be," I said.

Susan's big, dark eyes seemed intensely alive to me. Pearl rested her long chin on the table, and Susan patted her absently, smoothing Pearl's ears.

"You have to help him," she said.

"I guess I do," I said.

43

—•—

HAWK AND I were in Marshport, in a badly stocked bodega a half block up from the mouth of a weed-thick alley
that ran between two paintless tenements. The alley opened
at its far end directly across the street from Rimbaud's office.

"What story was the Gray Man going to tell?" I said.

"Don't know. I just told him get a Ukrainian down here
at three, and let no one know he'd done it."

An uninteresting-looking gray Chevy pulled around the
corner and parked by the alley.

"Well, he thought of something," I said.

Hawk nodded, looking at the car. A big man got out.

"Guy with Boots," I said, "at Revere Beach."

"Fadeyushka Badyrka," Hawk said.

"Anybody else in the car?" I said.

"We'll find out," Hawk said. "I'll watch Fadeyushka."

We went out of the bodega and walked across the street. The Ukrainian watched us come. No one moved in the car.

When we were maybe five feet away, Fadeyushka said, "What?"

Hawk shot him in the forehead with a nine-millimeter Colt. The Colt had a silencer on it and made only a modest noise. Fadeyushka went down without a sound. *So easy.* I stepped to the car with my gun out. No one was in it. Hawk unscrewed the silencer and slipped it into his pocket. Then he stowed the Colt and picked up Fadeyushka and moved him without any apparent effort into the alley, down between the houses, and deposited the body behind some trash cans right across from Rimbaud's big plate-glass window. I knelt down and felt over his cooling body and found Fadeyushka's gun stuck in his right hip pocket. It was some sort of European semiautomatic nine-millimeter pistol. There was a round in the chamber already. Hawk studied the dead man for a time.

"I come in the alley," Hawk said. "He's there shooting in the window. I shoot, get him in the head. He fall back there behind the trash. Gun falls out of his right hand," Hawk nodded, "lands there."

"That's where it'll be," I said

"Okay," Hawk said. "I'll go in. I stand right in front of the front window, where you can see me. And I stay there until things are right. When I move out of sight, you shoot."

I nodded.

"The window is dead glass walking," I said.

"Then you head up the alley lipity-fucking-lop," he said, "scoot 'round the block and come running up saying, 'What happened?'"

"You already told me this once," I said.

"Never lose money," Hawk said, "underestimating your intelligence."

"Yeah, but I'm fun to be with," I said.

Hawk was looking at the office.

"Wait'll I move aside," he said

"Boy," I said, "you ruin everything."

"Don't call me boy," he said, and started across the street.

I stood beside Fadeyushka's mortal remains, holding his gun, and waited. Hawk went in the front door of Rimbaud's office. A moment later I saw his back through the window. There was no one on the street. No one but me and Fadeyushka in the alley. The people who referred to teeming slums maybe hadn't been to this one. I saw Hawk's back move left and he disappeared from view. I raised Fadeyushka's gun and fired three shots, as fast as I could pull the trigger, into the upper right-hand corner of the window. The plate glass shattered. The whole window disappeared in a cascade of shards. I put the gun near Fadeyushka's dead hand and sprinted down the alley. Out on the next street, I turned left. As I ran the block, I heard a gunshot. I knew it was Hawk. I turned left again and reached the end of the alley as Rimbaud and his two Hispanic cohorts reached it. One of them, Nuncio, whirled on me with a gun.

"I'm on your side," I said. "What happened."

Out of sight in the alley, Hawk said, "He with me."

Nuncio lowered the gun, but both he and Jaime watched me closely.

I stepped into the alley's mouth. Rimbaud was there with his gun in hand, standing just behind Hawk, who had his gun out.

"Tried to gun Mr. Rimbaud," Hawk said. "From the alley. Shot right through the window."

"Who killed him," I said.

"I did," Hawk said.

"My man was quick," Rimbaud said.

He looked a little rattled. So did Nuncio and Jaime.

"Was out the door 'fore I could even get my gun out, man," Rimbaud said.

"He was shooting from behind those trash cans," Hawk said. "He saw me coming and he, like, froze."

"Buck fever," I said.

Hawk looked at me.

"Don't call me buck," he said.

"Sho'," I said.

"So I able to drill him once in the head," Hawk said.

"You know who it is?" Rimbaud said.

He didn't seem eager to look closely at the corpse.

"Name's Fadeyushka Badyrka," Hawk said. "Works for Boots Podolak."

"The sonovabitch works for Boots."

Hawk nodded.

"Maybe Boots and Tony had a falling out," I said.

"You think Boots put him up to this?"

"Fadeyushka don't take a leak," Hawk said, "Boots don't tell him to."

"You don't even know him, do you?" I said.

Rimbaud looked cautiously at the dead man.

"Shit," he said, "I do. I seen him with Boots."

"I rests ma case," Hawk said.

Rimbaud stared at Hawk.

"Boots sent him," he said.

"Be my guess," Hawk said.

"Must have," I said.

"That mother fucker," Rimbaud said. "Wait'll I tell Tony. Tony will be bullshit."

Hawk smiled.

"I expect he will," Hawk said.

44

───●───

THE GRAY MAN, wearing a snap-brimmed hat with a wide brim, was leaning on the wall at the Wonderland MBTA station, reading the *Boston Herald*. Across from the dog track, Wonderland was the last subway station on the blue line, running north from Boston. Hawk and I walked down the platform and stood next to him. He paid us no attention. It was midmorning, and the station wasn't crowded.

"So far, so good," Hawk said.

The Gray Man kept reading his paper.

"Fadeyushka is dead?" he said.

"Yeah, and Rimbaud is blaming Boots."

The Gray Man nodded.

"When they find him," the Gray Man said, "the police will come at once to Podolak."

"And with a little help from you," I said, "Boots will blame Rimbaud."

"Describe the details," the Gray Man said.

Hawk told him.

"The window could have shattered in the exchange of gunfire," the Gray Man said.

Hawk nodded.

"This won't stand up if there's a real investigation by some good cops," I said.

The Gray Man smiled and looked up from his newspaper.

"Where would we find them?" he said.

"Good point," I said.

"Is the body easily visible?" the Gray Man said.

"No," Hawk said.

"Then discovery may not be imminent," the Gray Man said.

"Perhaps an anonymous tip," I said.

The Gray Man smiled his evanescent smile.

"Any theory on Boots's reaction?" I said.

The Gray Man shrugged.

"He cannot let it go," the Gray Man said.

He looked at Hawk.

"And the Ukrainians," he said, "whose number have depleted, will require revenge."

"You know that," I said.

"I know Ukrainians," he said.

"Racial profiling?" I said.

"I know Ukrainians," the Gray Man said. "And Marcus?"

"He don't like Rimbaud," Hawk said. "But it's his daughter's husband."

"I understand that she is not a particularly savory daughter," the Gray Man said.

"Still his daughter," Hawk said. "Tony can't let it happen."

"Besides," I said. "Both of them will think they've been double-crossed by the other one."

Hawk smiled.

"When in fact they double-crossed by us," he said.

"Which would annoy them both, should they discover it," the Gray Man said.

"And unite them in a common purpose," I said.

"Which would be?" the Gray Man said.

"Us," Hawk said.

"Fortunately," the Gray Man said, "at my end of the thing, we are not dealing with terribly smart people. How about Marcus."

"Tony pretty smart," Hawk said.

The Gray Man nodded, gazing across the platform at a young woman in a short, flowered dress.

"Well," he said. "That would be your end of the thing."

45

———•———

IT WAS MAY, and the weather was nice. Hawk and I sat with Leonard on the seawall that ran along Ocean Drive in Marshport, where the dark ocean stretched out to the east until it merged along the far horizon with eternity.

"Amazin'," Hawk said. "Dump like Marshport got such a nice ocean view."

"Nice," Leonard said. "Tony wants to know what you know about Boots trying to have Rimbaud capped."

Leonard spoke very softly.

"He tell you 'bout it?"

"He wants to hear your story," Leonard said.

"Lucky we was there," Hawk said.

I knew how fast Hawk's mind had moved between the question and the answer. Would Rimbaud admit that it was Hawk who had shot Fadeyushka? Or would he claim credit? Hawk decided that Rimbaud would be so scared that he probably wouldn't lie to Tony. It was the right response. Leonard didn't say anything, and his face showed nothing, but I could feel him ease up slightly.

"You the one aced him," Leonard said.

"Yes."

"You both up there to see Rimbaud," Leonard said.

His voice didn't inflect, but I knew it was a question.

"Lookin' for anything we could find on Boots," Hawk said. "Ain't no secret to you that we after his ass."

Leonard nodded.

"And why wasn't you in the office with Hawk?" Leonard said to me.

"Parking the car," I said.

"Whyn't you park it out front?" Leonard said. "Never nobody in that neighborhood anyway."

"Didn't think it would move our purpose along if Boots's cops gave us a ticket right outside Rimbaud's place."

Leonard nodded again.

"Gimme the whole story," Leonard said.

Hawk told him our version of the events. When he got through, Leonard nodded again.

"Lucky you were there," he said.

"What's Tony going to do?" I said.

"Didn't say."

"What do you think he'll do?"

"Didn't say."

Hawk grinned widely.

"What would you do," Hawk said, "you was Tony."

"Whatever Tony tole me," Leonard said.

"Okay," Hawk said. "I catching on that you Tony's man."

Leonard didn't say anything.

"You tell Tony that whatever he plans on doing 'bout Boots, we be prepared to help."

"Tony want to know first why Boots welshed on the deal," Leonard said.

"Maybe Rimbaud having too much success," Hawk said.

Leonard smiled for a moment.

"Probably not," he said.

"Tony send up some help?" I said.

"Brock ain't here."

"Where'd he go?"

"Back to Boston."

"Where Tony can keep an eye on him," I said.

"Tony got couple people over there."

"On the wharf," I said.

Leonard nodded.

"Bet Jolene likes that," I said.

"Jolene don't like much," Leonard said.

46

———•———

"I LET a couple guys beat me at pool," Vinnie said. "And I let a guy cheat me at blackjack. He had a fucking marked deck I could read better than he could."

"And?" Hawk said.

"Somebody owes me for the money I lost," Vinnie said.

We were in a pizza joint in Chelsea, with a nice view of the Mystic River Bridge. The bridge had been renamed the Tobin bridge about forty years ago, but I remain a traditionalist.

"I didn't hire you," Hawk said. "Speak to your employer."

Vinnie looked at me.

"How 'bout I pay for the pizza," I said.

"You was going to do that anyway," Vinnie said.

"What'd you get," Hawk said, "for all that losing?"

"Town's really organized," Vinnie said. "There's the vendors: dope, numbers, whores. Then there's block sergeants and section captains and the city boss, Ukrainian guy."

"You got a name?" Hawk said.

"Sure, but I can't fucking pronounce it."

"Try," Hawk said.

Vinnie shook his head.

"Naw, but I wrote it down. Guy spelled it for me."

He handed Hawk a cocktail napkin, on which was printed Vanko Tsyklins'kyj. Hawk read it and nodded.

"Vanko Tsyklins'kyj," Hawk said.

"Yeah, him," Vinnie said.

"He's the head of the organization?"

"On the flow chart he would be," Vinnie said. "Everybody knows it's really Boots."

We had a large pepperoni pizza on the table and were sharing it, except Leonard, who had a small salad and a Diet Coke.

"All the Ukes work for Boots. One of them's his bodyguard now."

"Lyaksandro Prohorovych," Hawk said.

"Sounds right," Vinnie said. "People I talk to think the other kid, Rimbaud, is a joke."

"He's a blackberry," Leonard said.

"Blackberry?" I said.

"Guy wants to be black," Hawk said. "Even though he look like a slice of Wonder Bread."

"There's an actual name for guys like that?" I said.

"Sure," Hawk said. "Guys want to be extra cool like Leonard and me. Natural rhythm, lotta sex drive. Hope their dick gets bigger."

"Nice they can rebel," I said, "and be down and funky and still not get rousted by suburban cops."

"Tha's right," Hawk said. "Want to be authentic Africans like me and Leonard, without paying the, ah, price of admission."

"And you authentic Africans don't welcome converts."

Leonard was looking at me silently.

"What the fuck he talking about?" Leonard said to Hawk.

"I never do know," Hawk said.

"Just hoping to bridge the racial divide," I said.

"Oh, that's what you doing," Hawk said.

"Rimbaud got any following at all?" I asked Vinnie.

"He's got a straggle-ass Puerto Rican street gang. Thinks he's gonna take over the city."

"How many."

"Varies, mostly kids, not reliable. People he can count on? Maybe eight."

"So Boots could swat him like a fly," I said.

"Sure," Vinnie said. "He don't have the deal with Tony."

"And maybe he ain't got that no more," Leonard said.

"Storefront where he was doing business burned yesterday," Vinnie said. "Somebody torched it."

"Whole building?" I said.

"Yep."

"Tenants?"

"Couple Marshport cops came through; herded them all out before the fire started."

"Guess the deal with Tony is void," I said.

"Hear anything from the Gray Man?" Leonard said.

Hawk shook his head.

"So what are we gonna do?" Leonard said.

Hawk chewed some pepperoni pizza, which seemed like such a good idea that I took another slice. Hawk looked sort of thoughtfully at Leonard while he chewed. Then he swallowed and drank some iced tea, and patted his mouth carefully with a paper napkin.

"Leonard," he said. "You got to decide something."

Leonard waited.

"You either with us or with Tony."

"I'm with Tony," Leonard said.

"We probably with Tony, too," Hawk said. "But if it worked out that we wasn't, I'd need to know where you stood."

"Be sort of depending," Leonard said.

"Yeah," Hawk said, "it would. I ain't got no problem with Tony. I don't want to kill him or hurt his business."

Leonard was quiet, watching Hawk.

"I am going to put this town out of business and kill Boots and the two Ukrainians."

"What you going to do about Tony's son-in-law?" Leonard said.

"Nothing," Hawk said.

"I ain't afraid of you, Hawk," Leonard said.

"You should be," Hawk said. "You should be afraid of me and you should be afraid of this slick-talking haddock with me."

"Aw, hell," I said.

Vinnie seemed totally immersed in the coffee experience. I wasn't sure Vinnie paid attention to anything he wasn't paid to pay attention to.

Leonard shook his head.

"Tony told me to stay with you," he said, "and help out any way you needed, and let him know what was going on."

"And if we got something going on we don't want him to hear about?"

"Be depending again," Leonard said.

"Sometimes not letting him know might in the long run be helping out the best way you could."

"That what it might be depending on," Leonard said.

Hawk looked at me. I looked back. He shrugged. I nodded.

"Well, we deal with it when it comes up," Hawk said.

Leonard was a hard case.

"If you can," he said.

"Oh, hell, Leonard," Hawk said. " 'Course we can."

47

———•———

"IT'S GOING TO go down today," Leonard told us in the parking lot of a donut shop on Route 1A. "Tony say he like you in it, but if that don't work for you, stay the fuck out the way."

"It work for us," Hawk said.

"Gray Man working in City Hall?" Leonard said.

"Yes."

"Might tell him not to," Leonard said.

"When does it start?" I said.

"You'll know," Leonard said and got out of Hawk's car

and walked to his own. Vinnie sat in the backseat, listening to his iPod. There was no way to tell if he'd even known Leonard was there.

"Tony going right for it," Hawk said.

"Seems so," I said.

"Going right after Boots," Hawk said.

"We want that?" I said.

Hawk shook his head.

"Gotta get the trust-fund money first," Hawk said. "And Boots be all we got for that."

I drank some coffee.

"'Less we can find somebody else to endow the kid's future," I said.

"Vinnie?" Hawk said.

I looked at Vinnie, leaning his head against the leather upholstery in the backseat of Hawk's Jaguar. His eyes were closed as he listened to the music.

"I see your point," I said. "So, we gotta rescue him."

"Is that a bitch?" Hawk said.

"It is," I said.

Hawk smiled and did a flawless Stan Laurel.

"A fine mess I've got us into this time, Ollie."

"Well," I said, "unless Leonard had a hidden agenda when he warned us about getting the Gray Man out of harm's way, we can assume it'll start at City Hall."

"Agreed," Hawk said.

"So there should be a lot of diversionary activity."

"Should," Hawk said.

"Which might work for us," I said.

"Always see the glass half full, don't you," Hawk said.

"A cockeyed optimist," I said.

"We engineered this sucker," Hawk said. "We can't just warn Boots ahead of time. We blow the whole deal."

"Hoist on our own petard," I said.

From the backseat, holding his earphones away from his ears, Vinnie said, "You know a petard is a land mine?"

Hawk and I looked at each other.

"I did know that," I said.

Vinnie shrugged slightly and put the earphones back in his ears.

"Hard to plan anything," Hawk said, "till we know what Tony going to do."

"We know he's starting at City Hall," I said. "Let's call the Gray Man."

"Okay," Hawk said. "You in, Vinnie?"

Vinnie opened his eyes for a moment.

"Sure," he said and closed his eyes.

48

───●───

THE GRAY MAN met us in the parking lot of a bait-and-tackle shop near the marina on Ocean Way, a few blocks east of City Hall. He got into the backseat of Hawk's car with Vinnie. Neither one paid any attention to the other.

"Tony Marcus gonna try for Boots," Hawk said.

"Where?" the Gray Man said.

"Probably City Hall."

"When?"

"Don't know," Hawk said. "Soon."

"Are you participating?" the Gray Man said.

"We gonna get Boots out," Hawk said.

"Out?"

" 'Fore he dies," Hawk said, "Boots gonna give me money for Luther Gillespie's kid."

"Ah," the Gray Man said. "Yes. You want it all."

"Un-huh."

"Do you need me to shoot, or can I help you better by remaining covert."

"Need you to get us in to Boots, or Boots out to us," Hawk said.

The Gray Man nodded.

"Without revealing myself," the Gray Man said.

"Exactly," Hawk said.

The Gray Man looked past Hawk at the boats in the marina slip. It wasn't much of a marina, and the few boats seemed to be mostly perches for herring gulls.

"Do we know the timing," the Gray Man said.

"No," Hawk said. "Boots got a private exit?"

The Gray Man nodded. He continued to look out past the shabby marina at the dirty harbor. From here you couldn't see the open ocean. You would have thought Vinnie was asleep in the backseat beside the Gray Man, except that his head bobbed very gently in time to the music only he could hear. *Probably emblematic of us all, bopping to the tunes only we could listen to.* I smiled to myself. *Crime buster/philosopher.*

"When the shooting starts, you think he'll use it?" I said.

"Boots don't scare easy," Hawk said.

"He doesn't," I said. "But he's not stupid."

"We need not decide," the Gray Man said. "I'll show you the route. You wait outside. When the shooting starts, I'll urge him. If he comes out, you take him. If he doesn't come out, you come in."

"You staying?" I said.

"Yes."

"You're more useful to us alive."

"I have been alive a long time," the Gray Man said. "And I have heard bullets fly quite often."

"Okay," Hawk said. "Tell us about the entrance."

"Have you writing materials?"

Hawk nodded. He took a pad and a ballpoint pen from the glove compartment and handed them back to the Gray Man, who drew silently for a few moments.

"This is the main entrance," he said.

"Here?" I said, "Where it says MAIN ENTRANCE, with an arrow?"

The Gray Man didn't smile.

"Yes," he said. "Around here, down along the side of the building on Broad Street, an alley cuts through between the old City Hall and the addition they built about ten years ago."

"Connected by an enclosed bridge at, what, the second floor?" I said.

"Yes."

"If he needed to, the mayor would walk across that bridge from his office and go down fire stairs in the new section that leads to a fire door in the cellar, which leads to a fire door that opens on the alley. But if you go down another flight to the basement level, there's a passageway that connects with the parking garage across Broad Street."

"Where are the garage exits?" Hawk said.

"One opposite the alley," the Gray Man said. "On Broad Street. One on the opposite side that empties out onto Exchange Street."

"Which is a main drag," Hawk said.

"On Exchange Street," the Gray Man said, "you are off and running. West on Franklin, north on Essex, south on Federal."

"Broad Street would just take you back into the thick of the firefight," Hawk said, looking at the map the Gray Man was sketching. "If there was a firefight, and if they surrounded the building."

"Only a fool," the Gray Man said, "would fail to surround the building."

"Tony isn't a fool," Hawk said.

"No," I said, "he isn't."

"Though occasionally," the Gray Man said, "I wonder about you two."

"So do we all," I said. "You haven't shared this information about the tunnel with Tony, have you?"

"No."

"Don't," Hawk said.

The Gray Man smiled gently and without warmth.

"I wouldn't think of it," he said.

49

SUSAN AND I were at a table by the window in the bar at the Ritz, looking across Arlington Street at the Public Gardens where spring was unfurling delicately.

"I think it was the English writer," Susan said, "E. M. Forster, who said that if he had to choose between betraying his country and betraying his friend, he hoped he'd have the courage to betray his country."

"The analogy is imperfect," I said.

"All analogies are," Susan said. "But it's suggestive."

"If I didn't help Hawk," I said, "I'm not sure he would consider it betrayal."

Susan nodded. It was 5:10. There was a lot of traffic on Arlington Street. People going home to supper and their families. Some probably happy about it. Some probably not.

"What would you consider it?" Susan said.

I poured a little beer from the bottle into the glass, straight in so it would foam. Beer tasted better with a head on it.

"Betrayal," I said.

She nodded again.

"But if you join him in wiping out Boots Podolak, you'll also be betraying something, won't you?"

A string of giggly young people entered the crosswalk at Newbury Street and froze traffic back to Beacon Street. The kids seemed to enjoy it as they ambled across.

"Me, I guess."

"I guess," Susan said.

With the cars still backed up, a shabby, long-haired man stumbled along between them, asking for money. He was wearing a red Nike muscle shirt, and his thin, white arms were thick with blue tattooing. Most people ignored him.

"You have any solutions?" I said.

"No," Susan said. "But I know what you are going to do."

I drank some beer and watched a black stretch limo discharge passengers into the solicitous keeping of a doorman.

"I can't back off," I said. "I have to stay with him."

"I know," Susan said.

"So why am I talking about it," I said.

"Because it's you and me," Susan said. "We talk about everything."

"What would you do?" I said.

"In the unlikely event that I were you?" Susan said.

I nodded.

"I'd stay with Hawk," she said.

"And you a Harvard girl," I said.

"And it would bother me," she said. "And I'd face the fact that I was doing something I thought was wrong rather than betray my friend, which"—she smiled at me—"would therefore make it sort of right."

"Jesus," I said. "You shrinks are really convolute."

"Whatever we are," Susan said, "we have talked enough to people who are in big messes to know that whatever you do may make you feel bad, but mostly, in time, if you're tough and don't indulge yourself, it'll pass and you'll forgive yourself."

"Cynical, too," I said.

"I think that's hopeful, that unless you're obsessive you'll forgive yourself," Susan said. "It's also the truth."

"The truth will set you free?" I said.

Susan nodded.

"And make you cynical," she said.

The traffic had thinned on Arlington Street. Most of the people heading home from work were on Storrow Drive by now. Or the pike. Or the expressway. Or the tunnels. Or the

Zakim Bridge. Some were home by now, having their first drink before dinner. Maybe looking at the paper. Probably none of them were planning to shoot it out with a bunch of Ukrainian sociopaths. Susan turned her wineglass slowly on the tabletop in front of her. I put my hands out, and she let go of the glass and took them.

"Thanks," I said.

"You're welcome," she said. "Now I want to vent, briefly."

"Fair's fair," I said.

"If you let yourself get killed, I will want to die too," she said.

I nodded. It felt as if I needed more air in my chest. The waiter brought us new drinks. Outside the window, a door-man put two fingers in his mouth and whistled down a cab. I had always wished I could do that whistle, but I never could. I inhaled a lot of air as quietly as I could. I didn't want to be caught sighing.

"So far, so good," I said.

Susan smiled.

"Yes," she said. "So far, very good."

50

———•———

"SHOOTING START TODAY," Hawk said.

"Leonard tell you?"

"Yep."

"Tell you the time?"

"Nope."

We were in Hawk's car, parked at the curb in the little square that fronted City Hall. It was 7 A.M. on a May morning, and even Marshport had a fresh May morning quality as we sipped our coffee and watched the few people employed in Marshport straggle along to work.

"My guess is soon," I said.

"Ford Expedition?" Hawk said. "On the corner?"

"Yes."

"Best I could see through the tinted glass," Hawk said, "there be several aggressive-looking brothers in there."

"Car's black, too," I said.

"As it should be," Hawk said.

"Bet there's some more around," I said.

"Blue Town Car over there," Hawk said. "Other corner."

"And maybe a couple back of the building."

"Pretty sure," Hawk said. "Vinnie's back there, case things go that way."

"With cell phone?" I said.

"Un-huh."

"How did we crime busters function without them all those years?"

"Yelled loud," Hawk said.

"You know what I like here?" I said. "There's a bunch of black guys waiting in cars to shoot it up with a bunch of white guys, and it's not about race."

"Be about power and money, mostly," Hawk said.

"Race can't hold a candle," I said.

"What can?" Hawk said.

We drank some coffee. Nobody did anything. The Expedition and the Town Car sat quietly.

"Gray Man know?" I said.

"Un-huh."

At eight o'clock, a few public servants began to drift into City Hall.

"They waiting for Boots to arrive," Hawk said.

"If they don't spot him when he arrives, how will they know he's there?" I said. "He might come in through his private tunnel."

"Whenever go time is, they go," Hawk said. "He ain't in there, they shoot somebody else. Be an object lesson."

"Lot of people to shoot," I said.

Hawk shook his head.

"Leonard running this," Hawk said. "He pretty slick. He know Tony don't like to shoot civilians. Civilians stay down and out the way, they be safe enough."

"Hiding behind a desk in the middle of a shootout is not what everyone would consider safe."

Hawk smiled.

"Things be relative," he said.

"Tony has Leonard running it," I said.

"Un-huh. Tony pretty good with a gun, and he ain't scared of much, but he know who he is and what he do best, and he know how to delegate. Leonard can run this."

"And he wouldn't send Ty Bop or Junior," I said. "They're specialists."

"They belong to Tony. Junior will stomp somebody if Tony tells him, and Ty Bop shoot who Tony tell him. But they main work is protecting Tony."

"Like a closer," I said.

"Un-huh."

"Age of specialization," I said.

We had some more coffee. Whoever was going to work appeared to have gone. The square was quiet. At 9:35, a small procession arrived at City Hall. A police van pulled up, and some SWAT types got out with automatic weapons and spread out in front of City Hall. Then a limo pulled up and Boots got out and walked up the front steps and into City Hall with a Ukrainian on either side of him, and four uniformed cops around them. The SWAT types got back in the van and the van pulled away.

At 10:00 Leonard and five other men got out of the Expedition. One of the men carried a shoulder bag. They walked across the square and into City Hall.

"Here we go," I said.

Hawk nodded.

"Good," Hawk said. "'Cause we out of coffee."

"They're wearing some Kevlar," I said. "But I don't see heavy weapons."

"Something in the bag," Hawk said.

"Grenades, maybe?"

"Maybe," Hawk said. "Maybe something disassembled."

"Maybe ammo," I said.

"Be prepared," Hawk said.

We heard a single gunshot from City Hall. It wasn't very loud and, muffled by the building, it didn't sound like much of anything unless you were listening for it.

"Be the cop in the lobby," Hawk said.

Hawk's cell phone doubled as a car phone. It rang.

We heard three more shots.

Hawk pressed the speaker button.

"Yo," he said.

The Gray Man said, "They are in the building. I've encouraged Podolak to exit through the tunnel. The Ukrainians will take him."

"Car?"

"Yes, in the garage, a silver Volvo SUV."

"Exchange Street exit?"

"Almost certainly."

"You?"

I could almost hear the Gray Man's mirthless, wispy smile.

"I have my own plans," he said. "We'll talk again."

The connection broke. Hawk pressed the end button and put the car in gear, and we drove around the square and a block up, where we could see the Exchange Street exit from the garage. We were far enough away so that the gunfire, which had become more frequent, was a barely audible sequence of pops. A block from the field of fire, you wouldn't know anything was up. In the distance, I could hear a siren.

"Reinforcements," I said.

"My guess," Hawk said, "they going to run into some sort of roadblock 'fore they get here. I tole you. Leonard's pretty slick."

As he spoke, the silver Volvo SUV came out of the garage and went west on Franklin Street.

"Tally ho," Hawk said, and we drove along Franklin Street behind them.

51

HAWK COULD TAIL a fox through a henhouse, and neither the fox nor the hens would know it. While he drove
along, three cars in back of the silver Volvo, I called Vinnie.

"We're on Franklin Street, going west behind Boots," I said.
"You should probably go home before somebody shoots you."

Vinnie said "Sure," and broke the connection.

"Vinnie don't say much," Hawk said.

"You wish he'd talk more?" I said.

"God, no," Hawk said.

We went through Saugus and up Route 1. We went east on Route 128 and south on 114.

"We seem to be moving in a large circle," I said.

"Be safer to go around the fight than through it," Hawk said.

"Plus," I said, "fooling anyone trying to follow."

"You bet," Hawk said.

After an hour and a half, we ended up almost next door to Marshport in the Phillips's Point section of Swampscott, near Tedesco Rocks, a bit beyond the foot of a long driveway that wound up to a squat little flat-roofed fieldstone castle with a crenelated roofline and a round tower at one end. The silver Volvo had pulled into that driveway and parked in the big circle at the top.

"Tasteful," Hawk said.

"Probably got boiling oil," I said, "ready on the roof."

"At least there no drawbridge," Hawk said.

We sat and looked at the house. It sat high on some sort of ledge. The ocean was below it in the back. There was land on both sides, between it and its neighbors.

"Got an entry plan?" I said.

"No."

"Good to be working with a pro," I said. "Assuming we get in, you got an exit plan?"

"Same as usual," Hawk said.

"Run like hell?" I said.

"That one," Hawk said.

We sat for a while more with the car windows down. It was a warm, damp, and overcast day. The kind of day that might feature a thunderstorm before it was over. A car passed us in the other direction. A solitary gull swung over us on its way to the sea.

"Here the plan," Hawk said.

"Oh, good," I said.

"We walks up the driveway and rings the front doorbell."

"Un-huh."

"Tha's it," Hawk said.

I didn't say anything. Hawk didn't say anything. Above us, the gull did another long sweep.

"Well," I said finally, "it's an easy plan to remember."

We got out of the car. Hawk opened the trunk and took out two dark-blue Kevlar vests. He handed me one. I put it on and adjusted the Velcro straps. Hawk put his on.

"Don't tell Vinnie we wore these," I said. "He'll think we're sissies."

"He don't have to know," Hawk said.

We started up the driveway. Hawk had his big .44 out and concealed behind his right leg. I had brought my Browning nine-millimeter.

"Put the gun away," Hawk said. "We get in, I take the Ukrainians. You take Boots. I don't want him dead."

"Okay if I tickle him?" I said.

"Long as he don't die," Hawk said.

I holstered the Browning.

It was a long walk up the driveway. Except for the easy long cycle of the seagull's pattern, nothing happened as we walked it. No dogs barked. No alarms sounded. No one yelled, "Hey you." No one shot us. Only the slow silence and the seagull. It was a white seagull with some gray. There are actually many kinds of seagulls. Maybe this one was a herring gull. Maybe it didn't make all that much difference what this one was.

At the front door, Hawk put his left hand over the peephole and rang the bell.

There was movement, then silence, then a voice said, "What?"

Hawk said something in a language that might have been Ukrainian. And after a moment, the door opened on a chain. Hawk and I hit it simultaneously as it opened, and the chain pulled loose. The door flew open, and the man who opened it staggered backward, raising a handgun as he staggered. Hawk shot him once in the face, under the left eye.

"Lyaksandro," Hawk said, as if he were checking him off a list.

We were in a high foyer full of heavy furniture. Two men appeared in the archway to our right. One of them was Boots, with a small handgun. The other man had an Uzi. I dove at Boots. I heard Hawk fire. I rammed into Boots and he went down. I got hold of the handgun and twisted it sideways as he fired. He kept firing. I kept twisting. The bullets splintered into some of the heavy furniture. He struggled to turn it toward me and failed. Then the gun was empty. He let it go and began to fight me. With my left hand, I got hold of his hair and rolled sideways, twisting him with me. He was flailing at me with both fists, but I was too close to him for him to get much behind the punches. He didn't have much of a punch, anyway. I put my forearm under his chin and pressed it against his throat. He tried to bite me. I pressed harder. He was having trouble breathing.

"Okay," he croaked. "Okay."

I took my forearm off his neck, kept hold of his hair, and got us both on our feet. Hawk was looking down at the man with the Uzi.

"Vanko," he said.

It was hard to hear him. The room still seemed full of gunfire. My ears rang. Hawk put the .44 away and looked at me and Boots.

"What the fuck?" Boots said.

"Shut up," Hawk said.

He looked at me.

"Bring him," he said, and turned and walked past the two dead men, out the front door, and toward the car parked down the hill.

52

───●───

WE WERE in my office. We had parked illegally in the alley and come up the back way and encountered nobody. I was sitting at my desk, which always ups my sense of self-worth. Boots was in a client chair. Hawk was standing between Boots and my office door. Boots was looking silently at nothing, staring out the window behind me, maybe contemplating eternity.

"What the hell was that mumbo jumbo at the door?" I said to Hawk.

"Ukrainian," Hawk said. "I said, 'Hurry up, it's an emergency.'"

"You speak Ukrainian?" I said.

"Memorized the phrase, case I needed it."

"Like you memorized the five Ukrainians involved in shooting Luther," I said.

"Names and faces," Hawk said.

"Remind me not to annoy you," I said.

"Too late," Hawk said.

Boots continued to stare blankly. He seemed smaller than he had been, and limp. Like an uprooted weed.

Standing behind him, Hawk said, "You didn't make a break for it, so I figure you hoping to live."

Boots stared.

"You hoping to live?" Hawk said.

Boots didn't answer. Hawk cuffed him on the back of the head.

"You hoping?" Hawk said.

Boots shrugged.

"Hard being tough when you alone," Hawk said. "Easier when some of your people around."

Boots shrugged again.

"You got a chance," Hawk said. "You do what I tell you."

Boots was motionless for a moment, then nodded.

"You give me ten million dollars," Hawk said. Boots was silent for a time, and when he finally spoke, his voice sounded as if he hadn't spoken for a long time.

"I don't have that," he said.

Hawk took out his gun and pressed the barrel hard against Boots's right temple. He cocked it. The mechanical sound of the hammer going back was harsh in the quiet room.

"'Course you do," Hawk said.

"I don't. I mean, I may be worth it, but I don't have that in cash."

"How much you got in cash?"

"Maybe five?"

Hawk looked at me.

"Marty Siegal told me, if you shop, you can get a secure three percent at the moment."

"Hundred and fifty thousand a year," Hawk said. "Think Rita will shop?"

"Somebody will," I said.

"Think one hundred fifty thousand enough?"

"Probably more than Luther made," I said.

Hawk nodded.

"How 'bout inflation?" Hawk said. "Kid's still a baby."

"Invested right, it'll grow with inflation."

"And Rita will invest it right," Hawk said.

Then he smiled and said in unison with me, "Somebody will."

During the conversation, Boots sat motionless and without affect.

"Okay," Hawk said to Boots. "Five it is. I find out you had more and you dead."

Boots nodded. His Adam's apple bobbed as he swallowed. It was the first sign of life in him.

"You gonna wire-transfer it to an account I'll give you. When the transfer is done and the money in the account, you free as a buzzard."

"I don't know how to do that," Boots said. "My accountant does that."

"Where you accountant?" Hawk said.

"State Street."

"In town here?" Hawk said.

"Yes."

"Well, then he probably still alive."

Without taking the gun from Boots's head, Hawk leaned forward and took the cordless phone from my desk and handed it to Boots.

"I don't know what to tell him," Boots said.

"Give him the paper from Rita," Hawk said.

I did.

"Routing number, account number, all that stuff," I said.

Boots was afraid to move his head with the cocked gun at his temple. He raised the paper so he could see it. Then he took in some air and dialed the number.

53

—•—

"IT IS ALL over the news," Susan said. "Says the whole town of Marshport erupted. Police came from as far away as Worcester. Governor put the National Guard on alert. Something like ten people killed; the number keeps going up and down. A fire at City Hall. The mayor is missing. The city is being run by the deputy mayor, somebody named McKean."

"The Kodiak Kid," I said.

"Who?"

I shook my head.

"I assume you know something about this," Susan said.

"Yes."

"I won't ask for details, but I need to know something."

"I'll tell you anything you want to know," I said.

"How many dead?"

"Since the beginning?"

"Yes. Since they shot Hawk."

"Counting Luther and his family, and the people did the shooting, and the Marshport numbers, maybe twenty."

"How many are you responsible for?"

"Depends," I said. "I helped Hawk set this up."

"Helped him, or watched his back while he did it?" Susan said.

I shrugged.

"Mostly the latter," I said.

"How many people did you shoot?" Susan said.

"None," I said.

"Good," she said.

It was evening. We were sitting on her front steps with Pearl, watching the action on Linnaean Street, at which Pearl was poised to bark, if there was any, which there wasn't.

"Responsibility is complicated," I aid.

"Not if you shot them," Susan said. "Then it would be simple."

"So maybe sometimes complicated is better," I said.

"I think so," she said. "How do you feel?"

"Uneasy about it all," I said.

"But?"

"But I did the best I could with it."

"Yes," Susan said, "you did."

A squirrel leapt with no apparent anxiety from a high branch to a low one. Pearl's large ears pricked forward, and her shoulders tensed. The squirrel jumped from the tree to a fence, and ran along the top of it. Pearl watched closely until it disappeared and, ever hopeful, for a time afterward.

"What happened to Boots?" Susan said.

"He wire-transferred five million dollars to an account at Rita's firm. It'll be invested on behalf of Luther Gillespie's surviving child."

"Does Rita know about investing?" Susan said.

"My guess is that Rita can't balance her checkbook. She'll have one of the trust lawyers manage it, and she'll godmother it."

"What will that provide for the child?" Susan said.

"More than one hundred thousand dollars a year," I said.

Susan nodded. We watched as two women with long, gray hair, one with it braided, strolled past us toward Mass. Ave.

"Is Cambridge the long, gray hair capital of the world?" I said.

"Un-huh."

"Great look," I said.

"Un-huh. Where is he now?"

"Boots?"

Susan nodded.

"Part of the deal," I said. "Boots comes up with the five million, Hawk lets him stroll."

"Just walk away?"

"Yep."

"So he's free and alive?"

"For the moment."

"For the moment?"

"Boots won't be able to leave this alone," I said. "Eventually, he'll make a run at Hawk, and Hawk will kill him."

"You're so sure," Susan said.

"I am."

"Why did Hawk let him go?"

"Part of the deal," I said.

"But why would he need to keep a bargain with a man like Podolak?" Susan said.

"Wasn't about Podolak," I said.

"No," Susan said. "Of course it wasn't."

"Hawk let him go because he said he would," I said.

"Yes," Susan said. "I understand. I just forget sometimes."

"You don't forget a hell of a lot," I said.

"Other than that, is it over?" she said.

"Not quite."

54

———•———

MARSHPORT WAS PEACEFUL. There were still some State Police cars parked at some intersections, and in Boston the legislature was discussing forming a committee to consider authorizing somebody to think about looking into what the hell happened in Marshport. Maybe. But for the moment, the horse parlors were in business. The numbers runners were hustling. The dope dealers were their usual active selves. Cartons of highjacked cigarettes were selling well off the backs of trucks, and somewhere, probably, Icarus was falling into the sea.

Hawk and I had walked peaceably into City Hall and up the elegant front stairway to sit with Tony Marcus and Brock Rimbaud in Boots's former office. Ty Bop and Junior stood silently in the hallway on either side of the door. I smiled at them as we went in. Neither of them seemed to notice. One of the big Palladian windows in the office was secured with plywood. The far corner of the big office was draped in polyethylene wrap. There were scorch patterns on the vaulted ceiling. The Gray Man sat behind Boots's former desk. Tony and his son-in-law sat in front of the desk.

"Mr. Mayor," I said courteously.

The Gray Man tipped his head.

"Things under control?" Tony said.

"For the nonce," the Gray Man said.

Hawk looked at me and silently repeated the word "nonce?"

"For whatever," Tony said. "Is it our city now?"

The Gray Man nodded.

"You going to run the town?" Tony said.

The Gray Man had his fingers tented in front of him, tapping his chin lightly.

"Until the mayor returns . . ."

Tony snorted.

"Or until a new mayor is duly chosen by the electorate."

"Or the city is in receivership," I said.

"But for now," the Gray Man said, and smiled faintly, "I am in control here at City Hall."

"So let's talk about plans," Tony said.

Sitting beside Tony, Rimbaud was jiggling his knee.

"You wouldn't be in City Hall," Rimbaud said, "wasn't for us."

Tony glanced at Rimbaud for a long, silent moment.

I did my always-popular Bogart impression.

"All the son-in-laws, in all the world . . ."

"What's that mean?" Rimbaud said.

"Means you need to be quiet," Tony said to him.

He looked back at the Gray Man.

"I want Brock to run the street business," he said.

Again, the Gray Man smiled fleetingly. Things amused him. But not a whole lot. He nodded.

"You met the supervisor?" Hawk said.

"You're so sure there is one?" the Gray man said.

"You meet him?" Hawk said.

The Gray Man picked up the phone and spoke into it briefly.

In a moment, a door opened to the left of the polyethylene drapes and a tall handsome man came in, wearing a good charcoal-gray pin-striped suit. He had a nice short beard with gray in it, and his hair was longish and combed back over his ears.

"This is Mr. Johnson," the Gray Man said.

"A fine old Afghani name," I said.

Mr. Johnson smiled and walked to a couch to the right of the mayor's desk and sat down. He crossed his legs. He was wearing low black boots with silver buckles.

"It is a name which serves," he said.

There was no hint of any accent. He spoke English with the regionless precision of a television announcer. He glanced at the Gray Man.

"Like Mayor McKean's name," he said.

"Mr. Johnson," the Gray Man said, "represents our Afghani partners."

"My duties are consultive," he said. "Enhancing the product flow, one might say."

"How's it been flowing lately," Tony said.

"It has been a contentious time," Mr. Johnson said. "But the product has flowed."

"And keeps flowing?" Tony said.

"So far," Johnson said.

"Because of you?" Tony said.

"All of us have helped," Johnson said modestly. "I try to stay in the background, not call attention to myself. As you might well understand. I am not comfortable making myself known to so many people."

He looked around the room.

"But the mayor insisted," he said. "And the nature of the current situation . . ."

He made a small, graceful gesture with his manicured left hand, the nails gleaming, and dropped it back into his lap, where it resumed being motionless. Calm. There is calm that's dense, full of stuff kept motionless. Like Hawk's. And there's calm which is merely the absence of anything else.

Like the Gray Man's. To me, Johnson seemed more like the Gray Man.

"The current situation is me," Tony said. "My son-in-law is going to run things for me."

Johnson's dark eyes rested silently on Brock for a time.

"Really?" Johnson said finally.

"Really, really, pal," Brock said. "This sucker's going to be a cash-fucking-cow."

Johnson nodded slowly.

"That's fine," he said. "Fine."

"So who do I see about product?" Rimbaud said.

"You would see me," Johnson said. "I'll have to modify the arrangement slightly." He smiled. "Change the locks, so to speak. Then I'll be back in touch with you."

As Johnson talked, Tony's eyes shifted back and forth from Rimbaud to Johnson to the Gray Man to me to Hawk and back to Rimbaud. Tony was far too cool to show anything on his face, but I suspected he wasn't comfortable.

"Then we're in business," Rimbaud said.

"We certainly are," Johnson said.

Rimbaud stood and put out his hand and Johnson took it. Tony looked at Hawk. Hawk didn't look back. Rimbaud pumped Johnson's hand for a time and then sat down, looking exhilarated.

"Will you be moving back into your office?" Johnson said, "on Naugus Street?"

"You bet your Afghan ass," Rimbaud said.

"Calloused, no doubt," Johnson said, "from so much camel riding."

"You fuckers actually ride camels over there?" Rimbaud said.

Tony looked up at the high ceiling.

"You'll call us there?" Tony said to Johnson.

"I will."

"Ask for me," Rimbaud said.

"Of course," Johnson said.

He stood and looked at Hawk and me thoughtfully.

"You gentlemen are not talkative," he said.

"No," Hawk said. "We not."

"The, ah, mayor, however"——he nodded at the Gray Man——"tells me you do good work."

"Yes," Hawk said. "We do."

"Well," Johnson said. "Here's to the new partnership."

"I'll drink to that," Rimbaud said.

Johnson nodded and smiled and walked out the way he had come in.

55

WE WERE ALONE with the Gray Man in the mayor's office. Tony had said not a word when Johnson left. He just jerked his head at Rimbaud and they departed. We all watched them go.

"Brock seems a lot more exultant about things than Tony," I said when they were gone.

"If this actually go down, then the Brockster be actually running it," Hawk said. "Tony knows he can't."

"But it's not going down," I said, "is it."

"I suspect Mr. Johnson understands Rimbaud's limitations," the Gray Man said.

"Ain't gonna see no more of him," Hawk said.

"Or you," I said to the Gray Man.

"Unless someone hires me to kill you," he said.

"Which one," Hawk said.

"Either."

"Hope they don'," Hawk said.

"As do I," the Gray Man said.

"Jesus," I said, "I may cry."

The Gray Man smiled his smile.

"I have no sentiment," he said, "and if employed to, I would kill you as promptly as possible. But I admire certain traits, and both of you have them in no small measure."

"Gee," I said.

Hawk said, "When you found Johnson, wasn't you supposed to kill him?"

"Ives had suggested that," the Gray Man said.

"Wasn't that why he gave you to us?" I said.

"I do speak Ukrainian," the Gray Man said.

"But you were supposed to use us to find the Afghan connection, and when you found him, you were supposed to ace him," I said.

"Yes."

"So," Hawk said. "You going to?"

The Gray Man shook his head.

"It would have ruined everything else if I did it sooner," he said. "And now"—the Gray Man shrugged—"he's gone again."

"And it pleases you," I said. "The way it's going to work out."

"It does."

"Hawk gets to clean up the people who killed Luther," I said.

"Except for Podolak," the Gray Man said.

"That will come," I said. "The city gets pretty well cleaned up of its, ah, criminal element, and Tony's kid gets to take over."

"'Cept there ain't nothin' to take over," Hawk said. "'Cause the Afghans have moved on, and when they come to ask you 'bout it, 'pears you done moved on, too."

The Gray Man said, "You sound like a minstrel show."

Hawk's voice dropped a pitch. With no expression he said, "I speak in many voices, my gray friend."

"Apparently," the Gray Man said.

"So there's Brock Rimbaud in charge of a business with no product, and no supplier, in a town that is probably going to be run by the state."

The Gray Man smiled.

"And you like that," Hawk said. "You like thinking 'bout the little twerp coming to the office and you ain't there."

"And trying to find Mr. Johnson, and he ain't there," the Gray Man said.

He put his hands on the desktop and pushed himself gracefully to his feet.

"So that's why you didn't shoot Johnson," I said.

"Certainly," the Gray Man said. "Even if I did, there would shortly be another Johnson."

I nodded.

"And Ives?" I said.

The Gray Man smiled.

"Ives expects to be disappointed," the Gray Man said. "It is the nature of his work."

He glanced around the damaged office.

"And our work here has not been fruitless," he said.

"No," I said. "It hasn't."

The Gray Man looked around the room again, then at Hawk and me.

"Down the road somewhere," he said, and walked across the room and out the same door that Johnson had gone through.

56

———•———

I SAT in my car in Roxbury, at the edge of Malcolm X
Playground, on a street I didn't know the name of. Across
the street, Hawk stood in front of a bench, in the playground, looking down at a very small black boy who was
sitting in the lap of a tall black woman I knew to be his
grandmother. The boy was the only surviving member of
Luther Gillespie's family. His grandmother was maybe
forty-five, strong-looking, with careful cornrows, wearing
jeans and a freshly laundered man's white dress shirt with

the sleeves half rolled and the shirttails hanging out. The boy pressed against her, staring up at Hawk without moving. He held onto her shirt with one hand.

Hawk spoke. The woman nodded. Hawk took an envelope out of his coat and handed it to the woman. She didn't take it right away. First, she took the hand that held it, in both of hers, and held it for a minute while she said some animated somethings to Hawk. Hawk nodded. Then she took the envelope and slipped it into her purse on the bench beside her. Hawk continued to look down at the boy. The boy stared silently back. Hawk spoke. The boy didn't answer. Hawk squatted on his heels so that he and the boy were at eye level. The boy turned his face in against his grandmother's breast. The grandmother stroked the boy's head. Hawk stood, nodding to himself. Nobody said anything. For a moment, none of them even moved. Then Hawk nodded again and turned and walked across the street and got into the car.

"We done?" I said.

Hawk nodded.

I put the car in gear, and we drove back toward downtown.

"First installment on Boots's money?" I said.

"Kid's money," Hawk said.

"Is there a grandfather?" I said.

We turned onto Washington Street. The black neighborhoods stretched out on either side, neither elegant nor decrepit. Simply low-end urban housing that looked like any of the other neighborhoods in the city, except everyone was black. Except me.

"No," Hawk said. "She lives with her sisters."

"She work?" I said.

"Yes."

"Sisters take care of the kid?"

"Yes. Kid's great-aunts. One of them is twenty-nine."

"The aunts okay?" I said.

"Think so," Hawk said. "They ain't, I'll see about it."

I nodded.

"They'll be okay. What was all the conversation about?"

"I telling her how much she get and when it would come and who to call if it don't."

"You," I said.

"Un-huh," Hawk said. "Or you."

"Me," I said. "Anything I should know?"

"Kid's name is Richard Luther Gillespie," Hawk said. "I tole him, tole his grandmother really, that he ain't got a father and he ain't got a grandfather. But he got me."

"Jesus," I said.

"I know. Little surprised myself. And I say to them, if something happen to me, he got you."

"He ain't heavy . . ." I said.

"Yeah, yeah," Hawk said.

He handed me a small index card.

"Grandmother's name is Melinda Rose," he said. "It's all on there. Address. Phone number. She got yours."

I nodded.

"I don't want him calling me Grampy," I said.

"Probably won't," Hawk said.

57

It was 7:30 on a chilly overcast Tuesday. We were at a table at Excelsior, with windows on two sides. We had a table in the back, away from everybody else. Cecile in the middle, Susan on one side, me on the other. Hawk across from Cecile.

"This is by way of a good-bye, I guess," Cecile said.

Hawk was watching the bubbles drift up in his champagne glass.

"I've taken a job at the Cleveland Clinic," Cecile said.

The menu had a gentleman's steak and a lady's steak listed. The lady's steak sounded better to me.

"An offer you couldn't refuse?" Susan said.

"Sort of," Cecile said.

She glanced at Hawk.

"And I . . . needed a change of scenery, I guess," Cecile said.

I knew Susan was fighting it, and I knew she was going to lose. She couldn't help herself. She had to try to help.

"Hawk?" Susan said.

"Yes?" Hawk said.

"I assume you are not moving to Cleveland," Susan said.

There was a glitter of self-mockery in Hawk's look.

He said, "My work be here, Susan."

Cecile was studying the menu. I wondered what she thought about the gentleman's and lady's steaks.

"So many to kill," Cecile said softly without looking up. "So little time."

Hawk looked at me.

"What that line about honor?" Hawk said. "From a poem?"

"Richard Lovelace?" I said. "'I could not love thee half as much, loved I not honor more?'"

Hawk nodded.

"Oh, spare me," Cecile said.

Hawk nodded thoughtfully.

"Cecile," he said. "You know, and I know, and they know, you got a nice offer in Cleveland, but that you going because you mad at me for not being who you want me to be."

"I'm not mad, damn it," Cecile said. "I love you, and I can't stand that I can't have you."

"Not good dinner conversation," Hawk said. "But it's on the table. If you love *me,* you could have *me.* You love somebody else and insist I be him."

"Oh, shit," Cecile said.

She looked at Susan.

"You understand."

Susan nodded. I was hoping she would settle for the nod. But she couldn't.

"I do understand," Susan said. "But I'm not sure that means I agree."

"You don't think I should go to Cleveland?" Cecile said. She was finishing her second martini.

"I'm sorry to sound shrinky," Susan said, "but I think you should do what's in your best interest. Given who you are and what you need, it may very well be in your best interest to end it with Hawk."

"But?" Cecile said.

"But it's probably important to see that it is your doing, not his."

"What difference does it make?" Cecile said. "He won't change."

"Probably can't change; neither can you. But if you blame him, you'll feel victimized all your life."

Cecile caught the waiter's eye and ordered a third martini. She was silent while he got it. None of the rest of us said anything. *Party hearty!*

"I never quite saw that part," she said finally, after she'd gotten under way on the third martini. "He can't be what I want him to be, and I can't not want it."

Susan nodded.

"If I could change," Cecile said to Hawk, "what would you want?"

Hawk shook his head.

"Nothing," he said. "I don't mind you want me to be things I'm not. You don't change, I don't change. Be fine, long as we don't fight about it."

Cecile stared at him, then back to Susan. She nodded her head toward me.

"Would you change him?"

"Of course," Susan said. "If it were convenient. And I'm sure he would change me."

She smiled at me.

"In fact, I guarantee you that right now he thinks I shouldn't be butting in here."

"Good call," I said.

"But you don't change each other," Cecile said. "And you do things the other doesn't like. And yet here you are."

"That's probably why they call it love," Susan said.

Cecile said nothing. We all joined her. She picked up her martini glass and drank some and looked at the rest of us for a moment and put the glass down. She looked like she might cry.

"I'm sorry," she said. "I don't mean to be rude. But I have to go."

Nobody said anything. Cecile stood and patted my shoulder as she went by, and let her hand trail over Hawk's as she passed him, and then she was gone around the corner and down the stairs. Hawk didn't look after her. He took in a long breath and let it out slowly.

"We having fun yet?" he said.

58

I WAS HITTING the speed bag at the Harbor Health Club, and Hawk was hitting the body bag. Every few minutes, we would switch. Both of us were wet with sweat and breathing deeply when Vinnie Morris came in. He leaned against the wall, watching us with his arms folded until we took a break.

"I been talking with Gino Fish," Vinnie said. "You know I used to work with him."

"I do," I said.

"You remember that, don't you, Hawk? I was with Gino?"

"Un-huh."

"Used to be with Broz, too, but we didn't get along. Got along with Gino okay."

Hawk was wiping the sweat off his face with a towel.

"That's nice, Vinnie," Hawk said. "Nice that you got along."

"Anyway, what I'm telling you is I don't work with him anymore, but we stay in touch. You know? Sometimes I do a little something for him."

I sat on a bench and draped the towel over my shoulders.

"Every little bit helps," I said.

"Yeah," Vinnie said, "sure. So he tells me stuff, sometimes, when I see him."

"Like what?" I said.

"Like he told me that Boots is around, blowing how he gonna kill Hawk," Vinnie said.

Hawk looked up.

"Boots is saying you ain't got the balls to stand up to him man to man."

"Man to man?" Hawk said. "Christ."

"I know," Vinnie said. "I'm just repeating Boots. Says he gonna kill you. And he's a pretty nasty bastard."

Hawk nodded.

"You got any thoughts?" Hawk said.

"I thought maybe I'd hang around," Vinnie said.

Hawk nodded.

"Now I got two of you," he said. "Spenser been hanging around since Marshport closed."

"All for one," I said. "One for all."

"*Oui*," Hawk said. "You think Gino might know where Boots is?"

"Why'd you say 'we'?" Vinnie said.

"French humor," Hawk said. "Think we should talk with Gino?"

"Boots tole Gino—actually, he didn't tell Gino, he tole a guy who knew a guy, you know, and it got to Gino. Boots says you got the balls, he'll meet you any day at the Marshport Mall, early, five A.M., when nobody's there."

"Empty mall on Route One-A?" Hawk said.

"Yeah. Been closed for like eight years."

"I'm supposed to go down there every morning until I see him?" Hawk said.

"Says call his cell phone and leave a message. Tell him what day. Come alone."

"No seconds?" Hawk said.

"Seconds?"

"Like in a duel," I said.

Vinnie nodded as if he'd known it all along.

"Sure, seconds," he said. "I don't think Boots got no seconds. Most people don't like Boots."

"I heard that," Hawk said.

"I figure me and Spenser go along," Vinnie said, "you decide to go, be sure everything is kosher, you know?"

Hawk nodded. He seemed barely to be listening to Vinnie. "Got the phone number?"

"Gino gave it to me," Vinnie said. "Write it on the back of his business card."

Hawk put out a hand. Vinnie took a card out of his shirt pocket. On the front in small, black lowercase raised lettering, it said GINO FISH. On the back in a small hand was written a phone number. Hawk took the card and walked out of the boxing room to the front desk. He smiled at the young woman at the desk, reached over, picked up the phone, and dialed the number. Vinnie and I came out behind him and listened. He was silent while the phone rang and the voicemail message was delivered and the sound of the tone was heard.

"Tomorrow," Hawk said into the phone. "Saturday, May fifteenth, at five in the morning."

He hung up.

"Man," Vinnie said, "you don't fuck around."

Hawk nodded.

"Early," I said.

Hawk nodded again.

"How you want this to go?" I said.

"I go there at five, he's there, I kill him."

"We could be cuter than that," I said. "We could go down there two or three in the morning, set up. Me and Vinnie, probably Leonard if we wanted. Cut him down the minute he shows."

Hawk shook his head.

"Come down and watch if you want to," Hawk said. "But that's all."

I looked at him for maybe thirty seconds, which is a long look when nobody's saying anything. Then I got it.

"He's got to try and kill you, doesn't he."

Hawk nodded.

"What the fuck you talking about?" Vinnie said.

"He needs to make a run at me," Hawk said.

Vinnie looked at Hawk without understanding.

"Vinnie," I said. "When we had Boots, Hawk made a deal. Boots gives five million to Luther Gillespie's kid, Hawk won't kill him."

"And Boots done that?" Vinnie said.

"Yes."

"So what," Vinnie said. "Everybody knows Boots is a scumbag. You don't have to keep your word to him."

"I can do both," Hawk said. "I can keep my word and kill him, too. All he got to do is make a try on me."

"Might be a little too fine a point being made here," I said.

"Got nothing else to make a fine point about," Hawk said.

59

I LEFT HAWK and Vinnie drinking beer in Henry's office and drove up to Marshport. It was after six when I got there, fighting the commuter traffic all the way. The Marshport Mall sat on a landfill dumped at the edge of the salt marshes where the Squamos River ran into Marshport Harbor. The landfill hadn't been as stable as everyone had hoped, and as it shifted, the buildings of the mall shifted with it, causing cracks and leaks. Doors jammed. Windows didn't open properly. Plumbing leaked. Finally, the place folded and everybody but the people who'd sold them the land lost all they had. No one wanted to build again on the land. No one wanted to spend their money to tear down the mall. So it remained a rotting, ambling, and spectacular eyesore as you entered Marshport from the south.

The hot top of the parking lot was distorted with frost heaves and potholes. I drove across it and parked next to the disreputable south entrance, took a flashlight from the console, and walked over for a look. The big glass doors were stuck ajar. Leaves and litter had blown in through them and fanned out for ten or fifteen feet inside. It was still daylight in mid-May, but inside the empty mall it was dim. I walked through slowly, moving the flashlight around. Some of the ceilings had collapsed. Plaster dust punctuated with pink scraps of insulation covered most of the floor. Glass from broken light fixtures and display windows made the footing uneven and raspy. The skeletal bones of commerce past were all that was left of the various shops that lined the central arcade. There was nothing of value left in any of them. I wasn't the first intruder. There were cobwebs and spiderwebs and empty muscatel bottles. In a corner of one of the empty shops were a couple of torn mattresses and some filthy quilts, where some of my residence-challenged brothers had apparently holed up. Another arcade crossed the one I was in. More of the same. Darkness, litter, filth, emptiness, and a million places to ambush somebody. As I walked, a large rat scuttled across the arcade and disappeared into what was once a shop selling evocative ladies underwear. I saw several others, bigger than squirrels, as I strolled. I spent an hour or so exploring the maze, and learned only that it would be a dangerous place for Hawk to enter. But since I knew he would enter it no matter what, the information didn't do us much good. I shrugged. *Readiness is all.* I followed my flashlight back to the car and went home.

On Saturday morning, I got up at three. Hawk would be at the mall at five, and I wanted plenty of time to wake up and drink coffee and dip my bullets in curare. At quarter of five, I pulled off of Route 1A and onto the scrambled surface of the Marshport Mall parking lot. It was light, though the sun hadn't yet officially appeared. At the far end of the mall I could see the silver SUV, parked near the north entrance. I drove to the south entrance and parked where I had twelve hours ago. I took a Winchester .45-caliber lever-action rifle from the backseat and levered a round into the chamber and let the hammer down slowly. I had the Browning nine-millimeter on my belt, but I didn't know how far a shot I might need to make. I leaned the rifle against the passenger seat beside me and waited. In the rearview mirror I saw another car pull into the lot. It wasn't Hawk's Jag. It was a dark blue Camry, and I didn't recognize it. I took the Browning off my belt and held it in my lap. The Camry drove slowly toward me. With the Browning in my right hand, I stepped out of my car and looked over the car roof at the Camry. The driver saw me. The Camry did a U-turn so that the driver's side was away from me and stopped maybe fifty feet from me. The driver got out and looked at me over his car roof. It was Vinnie. Each of us holstered our guns and walked out from behind our cars.

"Come to watch?" I said.

"Yeah," Vinnie said.

He went to the rear of his car and opened the trunk and took out a twelve-gauge Smith & Wesson pump. From a box of shells open in the trunk, he took a handful and put them in the pocket of his safari vest. Then he pumped a round up into the chamber and set the safety.

"Boots in there already?" he said.

"That's his car," I said and nodded at the Volvo.

"Hawk'll be here at five," Vinnie said.

"He said five."

Vinnie nodded.

"Gives Boots time to set up in there," he said.

"Yes," I said. "If you're not finicky, it's ambush heaven."

"I know," Vinnie said.

"You been in there," I said.

"Yeah. You?"

"Yeah."

"When?"

"Last night," I said. "After I left you. About six."

"I was up here 'bout eleven," Vinnie said. "Fucking place is rat heaven."

"Yes," I said.

Hawk's Jaguar pulled in and drove past us halfway to the south entrance. The Jaguar stopped, and Hawk got out and walked to the mall. He stopped before he went in and looked at Vinnie and me. He nodded once and went into the mall.

I looked at my watch. Five o'clock, straight up, as they say.

60

———•———

"I THINK I'll go sit by the other entrance," Vinnie said. "Since we're both here, might as well cover both."

I nodded.

Vinnie got back in his car, put the shotgun on the backseat, and eased the Camry quietly down to the north entrance, parking a few yards from the silver Volvo. I got back in my car.

According to the digital clock on my dashboard, it was 5:04.

The sun was above the far edge of the world now, and

the gray light had turned faintly gold. It didn't go well with the Marshport Mall. Hell, sunrise didn't go well with Marshport.

5:05.

A couple of seagulls circled the parking lot without much enthusiasm. Pickings were by now awfully slim, and the gulls seemed to know it.

5:06.

There was a thin fog lingering just over the salt marsh. The traffic on Route 1A was still desultory. Occasionally, a truck would lumber south toward Boston, but mostly it was just quiet. I felt as if Tex Ritter should be singing on a sound track somewhere. ". . . look at that big hand move along, nearing high noon."

5:10.

I took the Winchester and got out of the car and leaned on the fender. Traffic was picking up a little on 1A. Somewhere, somebody was frying something and making coffee.

5:12.

One of the gulls spotted something it considered edible. It landed and grabbed it. Two other gulls landed beside it and tried to get it away. There was a fair amount of gull squawk and flutter.

5:15.

". . . or lie a coward, a craven coward in my grave."

At the other end of the mall, Vinnie was out of his car, cradling the shotgun, leaning on the side of his car. The sun had cleared the horizon now, lingering brightly just above the gray ocean.

5:22.

One of the gulls had successfully wrested the scrap of garbage from the other two and flown off with it. The other two gulls had returned to the area. Maybe there was more where it came from. They circled slowly and low, looking beady-eyed and passionless at the littered surface below them.

At 5:27, Hawk walked out of the south entrance of the mall. He nodded at Vinnie as he passed him and kept on walking. Vinnie opened his trunk, put the shotgun in, closed the trunk, got in the Camry, and drove off. Hawk walked past his parked Jaguar and kept walking toward me.

When he got to me, he stopped and looked at me as if he'd never seen me before. I waited.

Finally, Hawk said, "Done."

"Boots is dead," I said.

"Yeah."

"I didn't hear a shot," I said.

"Weren't no shot," Hawk said.

61

"AND THEN WHAT happened?" Susan said.

"We got in our cars and drove away. I came here. I don't know where Hawk went."

"And you didn't ask him what happened," Susan said.

"No."

"And Vinnie, when he saw Hawk come out, just drove away without a word," Susan said.

"He did."

"So neither of you know what happened in there."

"Boots died," I said.

"But that's all you know."

"All that matters," I said.

We were in bed together with our clothes off. Susan was lying on top of me, her face maybe six inches from mine.

"Will you ever ask him?" she said.

"Probably not," I said.

She nodded slowly, as if I had just confirmed a long-held suspicion of hers.

"Probably not," she said.

She shifted a little, moving her hips.

"I'm having a little trouble concentrating," I said.

"Really?"

"Aren't you going to ask me why?" I said.

"I believe I know," she said, and kissed me hard.

I believe she did.

SCHOOL DAYS

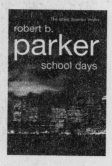

October 15th 2005: *School Days* straight into the *New York Times* Bestseller Charts at number 3

A troubled teenager accused of a horrific crime draws Spenser into one of the most desperate cases of his career. Lily Ellsworth is the grand dame of Dowling, Massachusetts, and possesses an iron will and a bottomless purse. When she hires Spenser to investigate her grandson Jared Clark's alleged involvement in a school shooting, Spenser is led into an investigation that grows more harrowing at every turn. Though seven people were killed in cold blood, and despite being named as a co-conspirator by the other shooter, Mrs. Ellsworth is convinced of her grandson's innocence. Jared's parents are resigned to his fate, and the boy himself doesn't seem to care whether he goes to prison for a crime he might not have committed.

To order your copy

£6.99 including free postage and packing (UK and Republic of Ireland only) £7.99 for overseas orders

For credit card orders phone 0207 430 1021 (ref BS)

For orders by post – cheques payable to Oldcastle Books, 21 Great Ormond Street, London WC1N 3JB or order online at www.noexit.co.uk

DREAM GIRL

'Nobody does it better than Parker...' *The Sunday Times*

When a mature, beautiful and composed April Kyle strides into Spenser's office, the Boston PI barely hesitates before recognizing his once and future client. Now a well-established madam herself, April oversees an upscale call girl operation in Boston's Back Bay. Still looking for Spenser's approval, it takes her a moment before she can ask him, again, for his help. Her business is a success; what's more, it's an all-female enterprise. Now that some men are trying to take it away from her, she needs Spenser's help.

April claims to be in the dark about who it is that's trying to shake her down, but with a bit of legwork and a bit more muscle, Spenser and Hawk find ties to organized crime and local kingpin Tony Marcus, as well as a scheme to franchise the operation across the country. As Spenser again plays the gallant knight, it becomes clear April's not as innocent as she seems. In fact, she may be her own worst enemy.

To order your copy

£6.99 including free postage and packing (UK and Republic of Ireland only) £7.99 for overseas orders

For credit card orders phone 0207 430 1021 (ref BS)

For orders by post – cheques payable to Oldcastle Books, 21 Great Ormond Street, London WC1N 3JB or order online at www.noexit.co.uk

ROBERT B. PARKER ORDER FORM

__978-1-84243-097-2	BACK STORY	£6.99
__978-1-84243-123-8	BAD BUSINESS	£6.99
__978-1-84243-192-4	BLUE SCREEN	£6.99
__978-1-84243-170-2	COLD SERVICE	£6.99
__978-1-84243-057-6	DEATH IN PARADISE	£6.99
__978-1-84243-216-7	DREAM GIRL	£6.99
__978-1-84243-167-2	DOUBLE PLAY	£6.99
__978-1-90198-291-6	FAMILY HONOR	£6.99
__978-1-90198-293-0	HUGGER MUGGER	£6.99
__978-1-90198-289-3	HUSH MONEY	£6.99
__978-1-84243-140-5	MELANCHOLY BABY	£6.99
__978-1-84243-159-7	NIGHT PASSAGE	£6.99
__978-1-84243-014-9	PERISH TWICE	£6.99
__978-1-84243-032-3	POTSHOT	£6.99
__978-1-84243-172-6	SCHOOL DAYS	£6.99
__978-1-84243-187-0	SEA CHANGE	£6.99
__978-1-84243-075-0	SHRINK RAP	£6.99
__978-1-90198-258-9	SMALL VICES	£6.99
__978-1-84243-116-0	STONE COLD	£6.99
__978-1-84243-058-3	SUDDEN MISCHIEF	£6.99
__978-1-90198-273-2	TROUBLE IN PARADISE	£6.99
__978-1-84243-059-0	WIDOW'S WALK	£6.99

Customer:

Address:

Date: Order Number: Credit Card Number:

Expiry Date: Issue No: Security Code (3 digit):

NO EXIT PRESS, PO Box 394, Harpenden, AL5 1XJ, U.K.
T/F: 01582 761264 or order on line at www.noexit.co.uk
(Cheques in £Sterling drawn on UK bank payable to No Exit Press)